ROSE BY ANOTHER NAME

by

Christine Karper-Smith

Marilyn,
A rose by any other
name may smell as sweet,
but love and friendship is the
sweetest of all.
Christine Karper-Smith
5-29-19

Cover art by Colleen Smith

ISBN-13: 978-0-692-17837-9

First Edition November 2018

Dedicated to my brother, John

No matter how happy or angry with me he is, John is always there for me. He helps me as much as he can, laughs with me at the silly things, and laughs at me as much as a sibling should. I've gotten through so much in my life because he was there supporting me.

Acknowledgements

Thank you to my dad - David Karper, Brenda Payne, and Lisa Blair. This book is possible because the support the three of you have given me, above and beyond. You've been emotional support, a sounding board, and have bought me food. (You know how I love food.) I can honestly say that this book would not exist without you being here for me.

To Mary Lindsey, you are always there to help me with a tiny problem or something I view as unmanageable. And almost every time, you're able to fix it for me.

Thanks to Stacy Eder, Mary Sinclair, and Erik Vinge for answering my questions.

Thank you, Tammy Pennington and Pam Van Allen for all the help, both writing and non-writing.

CHAPTER ONE

The yellow clapboard house stood like a sentry, protecting the yard around it. It hinted that the other houses were more loved. The well-manicured lawn contradicted it, but the cracked sidewalk that ran the length between the street and front porch confirmed its accusation.

As Skye stood at the curb in front of that cracked sidewalk, memories flashed through her mind. Perhaps it only reminded her of the house in the movie she saw last week. It had the actress in it, who was in that TV show and did the movie that was about the girl who was returning home after many years.

A cheerful voice yanked Skye from her reverie. "Are you here for the open house?"

"Umm, yes. Yes I am," she replied. She pointed to a sign in the yard. "Who's the girl?"

A large, white, wooden sign with "missing" written in red across the top, sat in the right corner of the yard. A toddler's smiling face stared out at the neighborhood. Rose Vandermeer, 3, was under the picture. It, also, included all the pertinent information: birthdate, height, weight, and to call 911 with any leads.

"Hello, I'm Stacy Lightner, the listing agent. She gestured toward the house like a game show hostess showing a prize. "So, would you like to see the inside?"

Skye nodded and followed the real estate agent across the lawn.

The front door opened as if to give her a welcoming hug. Skye's nose wrinkled at the assault of thick, sickeningly sweet air freshener. It smelled like a mixture of berries and lilies and made her imagine it as a cover up for a body hidden beneath the house. She brushed away the ridiculous thought as the woman shut the door behind them. *I watch too many police shows.*

Alone, Skye explored room to room, occasionally hearing the realtor speaking on the phone in the living room. She could picture the little girl on the sign playing in the room still decorated for a toddler with frilly pink curtains and matching bedspread. Her body filled with sadness when she saw the dining room. The table, which sat eight, had a small plastic flower arrangement in the center. A cartoon character divided plate, matching cup, and silverware designed for small hands, had probably sat in the same spot for twenty years. As if the little girl was gone, but her family wasn't letting go.

Skye walked into the living room. Stacy stood and smoothed out her slacks. Skye used her left hand to play with the fingers on her right hand. "I'll take it." Her lips curled into a smile.

"Fantastic! I'll let the owner know your offer."

Skye smiled as she nodded in agreement.

"There is one little thing." Stacy held her thumb and forefinger an inch apart. "It's a strange request, though. The owner has asked me to request whoever buys the house to keep the missing sign in the yard for another six months. It's not a requirement to purchase the house, though."

Skye wrinkled her nose. "May I ask why?"

"September will be twenty years since the girl was kidnapped. She wants it to stay up until then."

"So, this is the house where the little girl lived?"

Skye watched the color drain from the agent's face. She could hear the panic of a lost sale in her voice. "Yes, but it didn't happen here. This is a very safe neighborhood.

The last time the police were called for anything was a fender bender a few blocks away and that was months ago."

"I don't mind keeping the sign. So, what happened to her?"

The real estate agent didn't hesitate to fill the stranger in about the missing toddler. The signed paper was her ticket away from this albatross – none of the locals would buy it – and it was common knowledge in the town. "Her parents were in a horrible custody battle. They were treating her like a possession instead of a child. They both wanted her for the big child support payments. They weren't rich, but they were well-off. Her father's parents had big life insurance policies. He got like half a mil when they died. Her mother owns a restaurant here. One weekend, Rose was visiting her father. When it was time for her to come home, they both were gone. He didn't have any relatives, so no one knows where he went…or even if they're still alive." Stacy's face froze. "I'm sorry. I shouldn't have gotten into this. I'll give your offer to the owner. You'll hear from me when she decides."

Skye nodded instead of a verbal response. She waved good-bye with a flip of her hand.

Her feet moved as though she was walking in wet cement. Her racing heart echoed in her head. She knew she would soon be owning the home where Rose once lived. *This is the first step in finding the truth. Either I've just wasted my inheritance, or I've bought my family home.* She leaned on the roof of the car, after opening her car door, smiling at her soon-to-be new house. *There's no way she'll turn down $5,000 extra.* She slid into the driver's seat, gave one last glimpse out the passenger side window at her new home before driving back to her hotel room.

The key card didn't open her door. She tried a second time. Nothing. Skye flipped the card around, and finally, she heard the automatic click of the lock releasing.

Entering the room, she let the door close on its own. As her breath escaped her, she deflated onto the bed and closed her eyes. She wondered if her father would approve of her plan to find the truth. "He must have wanted me to search or he wouldn't have told me. But if it was just the pain medication, then there's nothing to find." She groaned in frustration. When she opened them again, the setting sun had warmed the stark white ceiling with shades of orange and pink as it snuck through the nearly-closed blackout curtains.

Skye dug her cellphone out of her pocket and dialed. She stared at it, knowing she had to make the call, but worried. She never doubted her grandparents' love, but they didn't like that she was going on an adventure to find herself…which wasn't really a lie.

"Hi Grammy." Skye's memory filled with pictures of her smiling Grammy giving her fresh baked peanut butter cookies.

"Hi," the voice on the other end sang. "How are you? Where are you?"

"I'm good. I'm in a hotel in some little town on the Gulf of Mexico," she lied. Skye's heart pounded. She had never lied to her Grammy before, but Skye didn't know how she would handle the truth.

"Are you by the water?"

Skye didn't have to lie this time. "Sort of…about an hour away." She sat up.

"Have you gotten to eat any shrimp? I know how much you love shrimp."

"Yes. I had some yesterday, but it wasn't as good as yours."

"You're just being nice. I'm sure the people on the coast. know how to make shrimp better than me."

Skye shook her head at the comment, as she traced the fleur-de-lis on the comforter. "Not yet. Maybe for dinner tonight."

"When are you coming home? We miss you."

Poppy hadn't entered her mind until now. *He'd support me finding the truth.* He was always her partner in crime. He's the only she told when she tried for the school play her freshman year, and he was the one in the front row for all six performances, applauding her one line as though she was the star of the play. "I don't know. I'm enjoying traveling right now. When I get back I'll have to start hunting for a job. I may have graduated from college, but I'm not ready to grow up yet. I guess that sounds silly."

"No sweetie, it doesn't sound silly. But it does sound like you're running away from reality."

Skye collapsed back onto the bed. "I'm not." She had known her dad was dying and had come to terms with it. She rolled to her left, into a fetal position.

There was a long pause before Grammy said, "I'm worried about you."

"I know you are. That's why I called. Really, I'm fine." Skye knew if she didn't cut the conversation off, she'd be stuck explaining more and more, but she wasn't prepared to explain the more yet. "I'm going to get some dinner now. Please give Poppy the big squeeze from me," the term they shared for a bear hug.

"I will. I love you, Skye."

"I love you, too, Grammy." The distance and the lie grabbed her throat. Skye fought for her next breath. She watched the screen go dark, after the call disconnected. She rolled onto her back stared at the white ceiling. Memories of her father flooded her mind while tears drenched her eyes. "I hope you forgive me for doing this Daddy, but I have to do it."

CHAPTER TWO

With the precision and efficiency of an air traffic controller directing landing planes, Skye choreographed directed the furniture delivery men with the furniture for her new house. "That goes there." "Upstairs, second door on the left." "Be careful with that one." When all of the boxes and furniture were in their appropriate rooms, one room remained untouched. Rose's bedroom was still how it had been twenty years earlier.

When she received the keys the day before, she walked through the empty house, transplanting the memories of her father from the home where she grew up, to the rooms of her new house. She cocked her head to the side when she got to the toddler's room. Everything was still in its place. Skye searched her memory for anything she saw in the room, but all she remembered was her room in California. A knock on the front door brought her back to reality.

Her heart pounded in her ears. She didn't know anyone in this town. All she had was her car, a new house, memories, and a secret her father told her. Skye scanned the eyes of every person she met to see if they knew her secret. Could the person who knocked know the truth and be coming for her? She stopped at the bottom of the steps, took a deep breath, faked a smile, then turned to open the door.

The brunette in a neon pink shirt on the other side extended her hands, revealing a measuring cup. "Here's a cup of sugar."

Skye stumbled over her words. "Umm, I'm sorry. What?"

"On TV whenever someone moves in to a new place, the new person goes to a neighbor to borrow a cup of sugar. I thought I'd save you the trouble."

Skye laughed.

"I hope I'm not bothering you. I live next door and wanted to say hello," the woman said with a smile.

"No, you're not disturbing me. I was just looking at the mess I have and wondering how I'll ever get organized. If you don't mind navigating a disaster zone, you're welcome to come in." She stepped out of the way to allow her new neighbor in. Skye wiped her hands on her jeans before accepting the sugar as she second guessed her invitation. She had to be careful of who she let in to her private world.

"I'm Sara Pierce. I live in that house." She pointed to brick house on her left.

"I'm Skye. Would you like to sit down?"

They headed into the living room. Skye shrugged, gave a crooked smile, and apologized as she moved boxes out of their way. When the path was clear to the sofa, she pointed less politely than she intended to the empty seat, then moved to the chair in front of the fireplace. "It's not staying here. It's where it was put here, and I haven't moved it yet."

Sara looked around and smiled. "It's fine. I understand. I'm sorry. I'm interrupting your unpacking."

"No it's fine. I needed a break."

"Are you from around here?"

Skye stared at the Pyrex measuring cup she still held. It was exactly like the one Grammy used when she made sugar cookies for her growing up. She took a deep breath and set the sugar on the coffee table. "No, I grew up in California."

"I've always wanted to visit there. What brought you here?"

Skye hadn't planned an answer for that question. She set the sugar on the coffee table. She used her left hand to play with the fingers on her right hand. "I wanted to try some place different after I graduated from college. I tore a map in half, so I only had the eastern half of the US. I threw a dart and it hit near here. I packed up my car, and here I am."

"That's amazing. I've lived here my whole life. I went to the community college thirty miles from here. I didn't even move out of my parents' house until I got married."

"So, it's you and your husband?"

"And our daughter, Abby. She's three."

"Would you like a drink? I don't have a lot, but can I get you Sprite?" Skye stood up and walked toward the kitchen. "I have some canned iced tea, too."

Sara followed. "Sprite's fine." Except for the cans of drinks, the refrigerator was empty. "What are you doing for dinner?"

"I thought I'd order something. Can you recommend some place?" She handed a can to Sara.

"No, come on over to my place."

"I wouldn't want to intrude."

"You're not intruding. You're invited. Tyler and I would love to have you. But speaking of which, we won't be eating tonight if I don't get back over there and start cooking." She set the unopened can on the counter.

Skye followed her to the door. "Are you sure about dinner?"

"I'm positive. Come on over in about an hour, or you can even come over now."

"I think I'll shower first."

Sara reminded her dinner was in an hour before heading out the door. Skye waved goodbye, closed the door then headed upstairs.

As Skye showered, she replayed Sara's visit. "I didn't see her do anything suspicious. She looked at me while we talked. She didn't look around an abnormal amount of time. I mean, she did look around some, but that's common when you're someplace you've never been before." She stopped shampooing her hair. "Oh great, now I'm talking to myself. Not only was my father insane, but now I am too." She started to rinse her hair. "Wait, what if she was recording our conversation, in case I let something slip." She paused. "Yeah, when I think that, I'm a few fries short of a Happy Meal." She finished washing out the shampoo.

* * *

Skye checked her watch again. She didn't want to go to Sara's house too early. If she went ten minutes early, that would be okay. It took her longer than she expected to get dressed, not being able to find the purple shirt she wanted to wear. But she was still ready twenty minutes early.

At ten minutes until six, Skye walked out her door. The front lawn was surrounded by a decorative fence, no more than two feet high. As she walked down the steps she wondered if she should just jump over the fence or go out to the sidewalk. She grew up a bit of a tomboy and jumping a fence was normal for her. She was told it was fifty-two feet to her property line in front. Skye walked to the sidewalk and around to Sara's front door.

A tall man with blonde hair and blue eyes answered her knock.

"Hi. Is Sara here?"

"Yes, she's in the kitchen. Are you Skye?"

She smiled. "I am."

"Come on in." He held open the screen door. "I'm Tyler, Sara's husband." He pointed across the living room to a little, long-haired brunette wearing a pink shirt. "And the beauty in the corner is Abby." The child didn't move. She was enamored with the doll in her hands. "Sare, Skye is here," he yelled toward the back of the house.

Sara came into the living room. They both said hello at the same time.

Skye complimented, "It smells good."

"Thank you. I guess I should have asked if you like spaghetti. It's not fancy, but it's food."

"I love spaghetti. Next to pizza, it's the best food ever."

"I think we are going to be best friends. I couldn't agree more."

After Skye offered to help and apologized for coming empty-handed, Sara told her to relax until dinner was ready. "You've been moving all day."

When dinner was served, Sara and Tyler brought four plates of spaghetti to the table. Skye stared at the pile of food in front of her. Her father always told her it was proper to eat everything on her plate when eating at someone else's house. That way they weren't offended, thinking she disliked what was served. "I don't think I can eat all this."

"Tyler always puts too much on when he's serving. Eat what you'd like but save room for dessert."

The dinner conversation flowed, and the laughter was abundant. Skye allowed herself to relax. *I haven't laughed this hard since before Dad died.* "These rolls are good. Did you make them?"

"No there's a bakery about a mile from here, Pinky's. They have *the* best turnovers."

"I'll have to check them out."

Tyler changed the topic of conversation to something which would include him. "How's the new house?"

"It's good as far as I know. I haven't slept there yet. In fact, I still have to assemble my bed before I can sleep tonight."

"Tyler can help you with that."

"No, I couldn't impose like that." The same fear she felt when Sara knocked on her door filled her body.

"It's no problem."

"I could use the help."

Sara added, "We'll walk over with you later."

"Thank you. That's one thing marked off my list."

"Anything else I can help with?" Tyler asked.

"I'm not sure. I have some repairs that need to be done: a broken hinge, a new countertop in the kitchen, some painting, stuff like that."

Sara pointed at Tyler with her fork. "Sounds like a job for JJ."

"JJ?"

"My brother. He's a part-time handyman, full-time firefighter," Sara explained. "He's really good. He made that sideboard."

"He's a carpenter?"

"More like a jack-of-all-trades."

"If he can help me that would be great." Skye smiled at the irony. She panicked at the thought of Sara and Tyler in her house but was willing to let another stranger in without a second thought. *If I keep thinking like this, I won't be able to guess my secret.*

"I'll let him know the next I talk to him." Skye nodded. "Ready for dessert?"

* * *

Sara held a pink pajama-clad Abby while she and Skye watched Tyler put the bed together. "I've got it. You two stay out of the way," he declared earlier. They were now enjoying him attempting to get it done by himself.

"Okay, quit laughing and someone give me a hand."

"I thought you didn't need any help," Sara laughed.

"I didn't say help. I said give me a hand."

Sara turned to Skye, "My hands are full." Abby had fallen asleep, her ring and middle fingers in her mouth.

Skye shrugged. "It's my bed. I guess I should help." She grabbed one of the rails to help Tyler attach it to the bed frame. He spent an hour building the bookcase headboard. Another ten minutes and Skye had a place to lay her head that night.

"Anything else you need help with tonight?" Tyler asked, dusting off his hands.

"Nope. This is all for tonight."

"We should get home so this one can get comfortable in her own bed," Sara handed Abby to Tyler. Turning back to Skye, she finished, "And let you get some sleep."

Skye walked them to the front door. "Thank you for dinner and for helping with the bed. I'd probably still be struggling with it - if you hadn't helped."

Tyler nodded as he spoke. "It's no problem at all. If you need any help tomorrow, Sara can help. I have to work." He smiled.

"Seriously, if you need any help, let me know. Abby is in afternoon pre-school, so I'm free between noon and three."

I am so tired. Please stop talking and leave so I can go to bed. "Thank you. I may take you up on that."

As if able to read her mind, Tyler stepped onto the porch. "You must be tired. We'll get out of your hair. C'mon Sara," he gave a nod to the side. "Let her get some sleep."

"You're fine." *Yes, please leave.*

"Ty's right. We'll get out of your hair. Promise you'll let me know if you need me tomorrow."

"I promise." They turned and walked down the steps and Skye closed the door.

The fourteen steps to the second floor stretched into twenty-four. At least that was what her legs told her. At the top of the steps, Skye took a deep breath, closed her eyes, and looked toward the ceiling. She swayed and grabbed the banister to catch her balance. Her next step dug into the carpet as though she was embarking on a twenty-five mile hike in the snow.

Her new mattress greeted her tired body. Even though she showered before dinner, Skye still felt sticky from moving. Building the bed didn't help her situation. "I should shower again." She looked to her left, where her clock should be. "Damn. I'll get it in the morning." *I have to call Grammy and let her know how things are going. I should paint in here.*

CHAPTER THREE

The sun forced its rays through the front window. There were no curtains to subdue its biting brilliance. Skye grabbed the pillow next to her and sandwiched her head between it and the one on which her head was lying. She continued to sleep until the sun poked through the other front window.

When Skye awoke, she looked for her clock which still wasn't there. She let out a quick breath. "I have to find that clock." Still dressed in the clothes from the night before, she made her way to the kitchen. Out of force of habit, she opened the refrigerator and cabinets. The only thing she found was cans of drink. She grabbed a can of tea, moved a chair to the table, then sat down.

Her life in Malibu seemed more like a dream than a memory. But there were two people who were proof that it was real. She found her cell phone, touched the number three, then the send button, and listened to it ring four times.

"Hello," the masculine voice said.

"Hi Poppy."

"Hello."

"How are you, Darling?" Skye could hear his smile.

"I'm good. How are you?"

"Doing okay but missing you."

"I miss you, too. How's Grammy?"

"She's good. She's right here and wants to speak with you."

Skye could hear the rustling of the phone before going through the same conversation. She hadn't told them she bought a house, only that she was renting -- they'd know she had no intention of returning home anytime soon. If they knew, it would break their heart. And she couldn't do that to them.

Her stomach told her it was time to eat something. After multiple failed attempts to get her grandparents to hang up, she told them she was hungry. Worried she wasn't eating enough, they let her get off the phone on the condition she got something to eat right away. A promise she wouldn't have a problem keeping.

Forgoing a shower, Skye grabbed a pair of jeans out of a box, pulled on a polo shirt, and laced up her favorite white tennis shoes. She knew she would have to find a regular place to keep her purse and keys. She was positive she would starve to death before finding them.

Skye drove the short distance to a diner. The two waitresses were leaning on the counter when she walked in. They both smiled and said hello in unison. Skye replied as she slid into a booth.

A waitress tried to hand Skye a menu. "Oh, I know what I want." She watched the people outside pass by while the waitress retrieved her turkey sandwich and raspberry tea. She didn't fight the memory of her and her father going to a dive dinner not far from the beach for brunch every Saturday. It didn't start out as brunch, but he wouldn't let her have ice cream before she ate lunch. So, she'd get a turkey sandwich and a chocolate sundae for dessert. Her dad always got scrambled eggs, two slices of bacon and orange juice, then enjoyed a cup of coffee while she ate her sundae. Skye closed her eyes and sighed.

There are people who like to eat alone and in silence. Skye is not one of them. She enjoyed a side of chatter with her meal. But the only person she knew in this town were Sara and Tyler…and she didn't know her well enough to invite her to lunch. *Maybe after I get to know them better.*

Without a conversation, she ate her sandwich faster than normal. She paid her check then made her way outside. The door had another two inches to close when Skye turned around and went back inside the diner. Her waitress had already cleaned the table. She walked over to her. "I'm sorry. I forgot to tip you."

"That's okay," the waitress smiled. Skye handed her five dollars, a dollar short of a one hundred percent tip. Before the waitress could ask if she wanted change, Skye was out the door and walking up the street.

She paused in front of the shop she stopped in front of multiple times since moving to Centerville. The For Sale sign called to her. She always dreamt of owning her own business. Her bachelor's in business management was the first step to realizing her dream. This knick knack and card shop was perfect. *I've come this far. It'd be silly to turn back now.* With her chin tucked in her chest, she entered the store.

A girl who appeared to be Skye's age stood behind a counter. "Hi. May I help you?"

"I wanted to speak to someone about the for sale sign."

"Well, it's about eighteen inches wide and twelve inches high and written in orange ink."

Skye laughed. "I like you. Who do I speak to in reference to buying the business?"

"That would be Marge, the owner. She's out right now, but I can have her call you when she gets back."

"That'd be great. Thank you," Skye replied.

The girl handed her a piece of paper. Skye wrote her name and cell phone number on it. She checked her phone to verify the number before handing it to her. She got a new cell phone three days prior and didn't know the number. "Thank you. Do you have any idea when she's due back?"

"An hour or two, I guess. I'm not sure what all she has to do, but I'll give this to Marge as soon as she returns."

Skye thanked the girl a third time and turned to leave. She stopped after a few steps to pick up a figurine of a man flying a kite with a young girl. After flipping it over to check the price, she turned back to the girl. "I have to have this." Skye smiled as another memory of her father penetrated her memory that day.

There was a skip in Skye's step as she walked back to her car. Her life was falling into place, even if her father's confession was a missing piece to the puzzle. She got into her car, turned it on and heard her favorite song on the radio. "Yes," she said with a fist pump. She drove home with the windows rolled down, the wind mussing her hair, and singing along at the top of her lungs.

* * *

Stretched out on the sofa, Skye watched a DVD on her laptop. The cable guy was coming in two days and she couldn't wait to catch up on her TV shows and email. But for the time being, she was content with the movie she picked up a few days earlier.

Her cell phone rang. "Hello"

"Hello, I'm looking for Skye Maxwell," the voice told her.

"This is Skye."

"I'm Marge Cole. I own Bric-A-Brac and More. I was told you're interested in buying it."

"Yes, I am."

"Well, I have two options. You can buy it complete with inventory or just the building. If you decide to take over the business, I can recommend Gwen, who you met, as a wonderful employee."

Skye laughed. "Well, I am hoping to buy the whole business, inventory and all. But I would like to see everything beforehand."

Marge agreed. "I understand. When do you want to come in?"

"Is tomorrow okay?"

"Tomorrow's fine."

They set a time, said goodbye, then hung up. Skye laid back on the sofa to watch her movie, a smile glued to her mouth the whole time.

CHAPTER FOUR

Two of the three things on Skye's checklist were done: she got a place to live and a job. She needed the last thing, find out who she was.

The building betrayed what it held inside. The Gable and Ell house had transformed from a home to the town's library. Other than the sign on the front lawn, it appeared no different than any other house on the street. Even the flowers in front gave it a homey feel instead of educational. Skye knew that was the reason she was brave enough to walk through the door and ask for what she wanted.

The brown-haired lady with gray highlights, smiled as Skye entered the library. Skye smiled back as she walked toward her.

"May I help you?" she asked.

"I'm looking for old newspaper articles."

The lady informed, "It depends on how old you're looking for. Anything less than five years old, you'll have to go to the newspaper's office. We have everything older, and all of *The Guardian*'s articles."

"*The Guardian*?"

"The newspaper that went out of business two years ago."

Skye's head bobbed up and down, "Oh. I'm looking for articles from like fifteen or twenty years ago."

The librarian led Skye to a line of computers against the back wall. She clicked on an icon before Skye could sit down. Two icons appeared. "One leads to *The Guardian*. The other to *The Gazette*. Then just put in the subject or dates you're looking for, or both, and they'll come up." She brought her hand up, then flipped it down. "I'm sure you know how to use a search engine."

Skye nodded as she grabbed the mouse. She typed in the information. She saw the toddler's picture staring back at her. It was the same picture that was on the sign outside of her house. Skye read the accompanying article.

Rose Vandermeer, 27 months, has been
abducted by her father, Connor Vandermeer, 26.
The girl's mother, Alice Vandermeer, 23, told the
police her
former husband took their daughter for a weeklong
visit to his home in Greenville.

When he didn't return yesterday as planned, she
called police after being unable
to contact him. Police went to his home which has
been vacated.

The article continued and pulled Skye in; enamored by the details of the kidnapping. *How can a parent do that to their child?* Tears filled her eyes as she imagined how the girl's mother must have felt -- how she still felt -- not knowing whatever became of her daughter.

A shadow fell on the computer screen. Skye turned and saw a man standing behind her. He lifted his chin in a hello fashion. He asked, "Are you her?"

Panic skated throughout Skye's body. Her head vibrated back and forth. "Her? No." She pointed to the screen.

His face twisted in confusion. "I know you're not her. Are you the one who moved into the house?"

"Yes"

"Cool." He walked away.

CHAPTER FIVE

Skye walked into Bric-A-Brac and More then did a Mary Tyler Moore-spin, but without the hat. It was all hers. Most of her money was gone, but she had a house and a business to show for it. Her excitement was swallowed by fear. She looked around the shop. Panic coursed through her veins when she thought about what she had done. She was a business owner – the building, the inventory, the employees were all hers. *Well, the employees aren't mine, but they work for me...and there's only one.* She smiled at her joke. *But I am responsible for all of it.*

Gwen entered as Skye reached the office door. She opened it but waited for Gwen to get to her. Still wearing the smile she wore when she awoke, Skye said, "Good morning."

"Good morning. I'm surprised to see you. I didn't think you'd be in this early."

Skye walked to the desk in the office and set down the box she was holding. "I wanted to get an idea of what you do to open, to see if you or I want to make any changes." She stood in front of her desk, using her right hand to play with the fingers on her left hand.

Gwen shrugged. "The only thing I do is start the coffee, unlock the door, and do anything Marge asked me to do. She'd leave a note on the register with a list. It would be stuff like price a shipment that just came in or clean the glass in any of the cases." Gwen walked across the room and stood in front of her.

Skye's head bobbed, acknowledging what Gwen was saying. She saw lines in Gwen's face she hadn't noticed either time she first met her.

"Is there anything you think I should know?"

Gwen thought for a moment. "Nothing off hand."

"Are you sure?"

"Yeah," she exhaled. "I'm sure."

Skye did not like confrontation, but Gwen's face told her there was something she wasn't saying. She searched her brain for a way to get Gwen to say what she was thinking but was at a loss for words. "I'd like us to have a great working relationship." *Too cheery, Moron.* "You really can be honest with me. I mean, unless you tell me you want to murder me, I think we can fix anything and work well together. Marge only had good things to say about you."

Gwen rolled her eyes.

"No, really she did."

"I believe that. She and I worked together for almost twenty years."

"Then what's the problem?"

Gwen crossed her arms. "Do you really want me to be honest?"

"Yes, please."

"Just remember you asked for it when you fire me."

Skye shook her head.

"I'm not looking forward to working for a spoiled rich kid who had Daddy buy her a business because she thought it would be something fun to do. I have to work if I want to eat. My wife and I work hard to have a roof over our head. I don't want to come to work every day and have to change what I changed the day before and end up hating coming here."

"No, it's not like that all. I'm not rich at all."

"You just happened to have an extra $100,000 laying around to buy a business?"

"Well, yeah…kind of." Skye paused. "I graduated with my bachelor's in business in May. I always wanted to own a small business. Two weeks after graduation, my father died."

Gwen's face dropped. "I'm so sorry."

Tears filled Skye's eyes. She never said that sentence out loud before. "Thank you. I paid for here and my house with the insurance money he left me. Now, I'm pretty much broke," she shrugged.

Gwen's hand found its way to her mouth. "I'm so sorry and ashamed."

"It's okay. You didn't know."

"You don't understand. I get so tired of people judging me and my lifestyle without knowing me and then I judged you without knowing you. I am so sorry."

Tears ran down Skye's face.

"And now I've made you cry. I really am a boob."

Skye explained that it was the first time she ever said her father had died out loud. "It's like it's true now."

Gwen wrapped her arms around her. "I understand. It's hard for a girl when she loses her Daddy. What about your Momma?"

Skye stiffened. *How do you know?* She wiped her tears. Her eyes searched Gwen's for a hint that she knew her secret. She swallowed hard in an effort to keep her breakfast down. "My mother died when I was born."

"Oh, you poor baby." Gwen hugged her tighter. "Well, you and I will show this town how a business should be run. Now, the only problem I've ever had with Marge was never having a regular lunchtime. She'd go out on an errand at eleven and not return until three. I was starving by then."

"Why didn't you order something?"

"She didn't want me eating where customers could see me."

She released Skye from the hug. "Then I can't see when anyone comes in."

"Well, from now on, you work nine to five with a half an hour unpaid lunch at eleven thirty?"

"That works for me."

"Then let's get to work. What do you normally do now?"

"Dust or stare at the door waiting for a customer to come in."

"Then show me where the rags are so we can get to dusting. This is going to be the cleanest business on this street." Skye raised her arm triumphantly.

Gwen looked like she had been fish hooked. "We?"

"Of course. I work here, too."

As they dusted the figurines, Skye would look at Gwen and wonder if she had given herself away; was Gwen now wondering why she reacted the way she had when asked about her mother? The world was playing Hot Potato with her life. She was waiting for the timer to go off and being forced to reveal the truth to some suspecting stranger.

CHAPTER SIX

Skye took a deep breath, then let it out slower than normal. The payroll – one check to Gwen – next week's schedule was done, and all the bills were paid. Now she could take the nap her eyes were requesting. She sank into the comfort of her new sofa. Her body tensed and released in response to the rap on the door. She peeked around the corner of the living room as she walked to the door. She didn't recognize the dark-haired man on the other side. She opened the door wide enough to speak to him, using her foot as a doorstop. "Yes?"

The man smiled. "Hi. Are you Skye?"

She knew few people in town. Three to be exact, four if she counted Abby. Her heart pounded in her ears, wondering how this man knew who she was. Or if he knew who she was. However, she did notice his smile. "Yes."

He pointed to the house next door. "Hi. I'm JJ…Sara's brother."

Skye exhaled the same relief as a few minutes ago on the couch. "Hi. Come on in," she said as she opened the door.

JJ took five steps in, looking around as he did. "Sara said you need some work done here. She told me it was okay to come over now. I hope you don't mind."

"No, it's fine. And I do need a lot of work done. No one has lived here for a while and it shows."

"Okay. What do you need done?"

"Do you want me to list it or show you?"

His grey eyes met hers. Like grey skies bring a chill, she felt her body shiver in response. But this was not a chill a sweater could fix. This was one that excited and enticed Skye as it warmed her body. "Showing me would be better. I'll get a better idea of what exactly needs to be done." He pulled a small notepad and pen out of his front left pocket.

"Okay. Follow me." She led him into the living room. "Some of the stones in the fireplace are loose. I'd like that fixed." JJ nodded. Skye walked into the kitchen. "I hate the countertop and want it replaced. Is that something you can do?"

"Sure." He nodded. "Do you have one picked out or have an idea of what kind you're looking for?"

"I want to paint in here. It's so drab. Do you paint?"

"I paint."

"Great. Then add that to the list." She watched him scribble "Paint kitchen" in his notepad.

"The countertop?"

"No, just the walls. I want a new countertop."

JJ tried to swallow the smile that attacked his mouth, but it won. "I mean, do you know what kind of countertop you want."

Her cheeks brightened as they filled with the realization of what she just said. "No, I don't have one picked out yet." Hoping to move past her embarrassment, Skye walked into the hall. "I'd like the dining room painted, too." She continued walking to the steps.

He took notes as he followed her throughout the upstairs.

When they returned to the foyer, Skye asked, "Is that too much?"

"When do you want it done by?"

She shrugged. "There's no rush. But I would like it finished as soon as possible."

"You do know I don't do this full time?" Skye nodded. "Okay then. It's not too much. I'll get the estimate to you by the weekend. Then you can let me know."

"Sounds good. Oh, I almost forgot the deck." Skye walked through the kitchen. JJ followed a few steps behind. She opened the back door, then proceeded out onto a landing pretending to be a deck. "This is way too small. Can you make it bigger?"

"How big do you want it?"

Skye looked at the clouds as she shifted her mouth to the right. With a shrug she said, "The same width of the house and eight or twelve feet long?"

JJ wrote something in his notebook. "Yeah, I can do it. But I'll have to bring in some people to help me. It's kinda hard to lift beams this high by myself."

Skye nodded.

"So, it will increase my cost by about…" JJ mumbled to his self, "Three guys, two days, twenty hours, ten times ten, one hundred times three, three hundred times two…" Turning his attention back to Skye, "…about $600 more."

"That's fine."

"Okay. Anything else?"

"No, I think that's it." She turned and led him back through the house to the front door.

"I'll have the estimate to you by the weekend."

"Okay. Um, how long do you think it will take you get it all finished?"

"At least three weeks…depending on how much time I can do it each week. But I can figure it out once you decide if you want me to do it or not."

Skye's head bounced up and down. "Sounds good." *And I wouldn't mind looking at you for three weeks.* She smiled.

JJ stretched out his hand. Skye grabbed it. When their hands met, it completed a circuit which ran between the two. "It was nice meeting you. I have to get back next door. I promised Abby we'd have a tea party before she goes to bed."

The smile on Skye's face broadened. She pressed her cheek against her hand which held on to the door. "Well, have fun. It was nice meeting you, too."

He returned her smile as he turned away. Her eyes traced his back and zeroed in a few inches below his belt. She raised her eyebrows and smiled. *Yeah, I could definitely watch him work around here for three weeks.*

CHAPTER SEVEN

After a short game of telephone tag and JJ making sure Skye understood that the total was only an estimate, he showed up bright and early the following Tuesday. Skye's mouth opened as far as the door when she saw JJ on the other side. His black tee shirt revealed more than the button down he wore the day they met. She was sure this tee shirt was centimeters away from restricting his breathing.

"Come on in." She wanted to hide the smile his arrival caused, but it was futile.

He walked past her. His jeans accented his butt. *No, that's an ass. No man who looks like that from behind has a butt. He has a man's ass.* She never had an interest in work boots before. However, on JJ, even footwear was sexy.

"Where do you want me to start?" He switched the toolbox he was holding from his right hand to his left.

"It doesn't matter to me. Whatever works best for you. The only thing I ask is that you don't do any work in my bedroom yet."

"Then I'll start with the fireplace and go from there."

JJ's grey eyes made contact with Skye a foot below her eyes. She didn't mind arching her back to give him a better view.

"Do you need me out of here by a certain time?"

"I get home about five thirty. But it's okay if you're still here. I go to bed around eleven. You don't even have to go home then." *Oh, please don't let him realize what I just said.*

"Thank you, but I should probably sleep at home until I know you better."

Skye's hand covered her mouth. She could feel the heat on the cheeks as blood rushed to them. "I didn't mean that. I mean, we just met, and…"

The right side of JJ's mouth curled into a smile. "I know what you meant. I'm just joking with you."

The curl hooked Skye and pulled her in. Having him spend the night wouldn't be so bad. She composed herself enough to tell him, "I left a spare key on the kitchen table. That way if you have to go out during the day, you can get back in. If you leave before I get home, you can lock the door and pull it shut, but please leave the key."

JJ shook his head in silent agreement.

Skye excused herself to finish getting ready for work. JJ was outside mixing cement in a small container when she walked outside. As she approached him, he said, "I noticed the paint's chipping on the mantle. Do you want me to paint it?"

"I'm not sure. Do you need an answer now?"

He shook his head. "Nope. I noticed it, so I asked about it."

She continued walking. "I'll check it out when I get home and give you an answer tomorrow."

He responded with a wave.

* * *

Skye sat cross-legged on the floor washing the front of a display cabinet. She watched as the wet lines dried behind her rag.

"You're going to wipe the glass away if you don't stop," Gwen said.

Skye looked around to see what she was talking about. "What do you mean?"

"You've been wiping that same spot for five minutes. If it's not clean by now, it never will be. What's on your mind, girl?"

"Just...stuff."

"Does stuff have a name, or do you only see him at the grocery store?"

The old, familiar redness returned to her face. "No, it's not like that." Skye thought for a minute. She didn't want too much personal information floating around town, and she didn't know how much she could trust Gwen. She also knew that seeing a man in a tee shirt was nothing to get excited about. *Unless it's a sexy tee shirt...a sexy black tee shirt...and tight jeans.* "What was I saying?"

"Not a guy, huh?" Gwen flashed an okay sign.

She lied, "I have to do some stuff for my dad's estate. I was thinking about that."

"Well, now I feel like a crap bag. I'm sorry."

Guilt flowed over Skye like a shower. She didn't like lying to Gwen and hated herself for pulling her father's memory into this, but it was his fault she was where she was. For the first time ever, she felt hatred toward her father. She thought for a moment, then decided that hatred was too strong of a word. Anger was more appropriate – pure, unadulterated anger. *Why did you do this to me?* Skye looked at Gwen. "It's okay. You didn't know."

Gwen changed the subject. "It looks like rain. Want to order lunch from the diner and let someone else get wet?"

Skye answered with surprising enthusiasm. "Oh yes. I'll get the menu." She jumped up from the floor. "I want to try something I haven't had from there yet."

Gwen followed her to the counter. "I know what I want."

Opening the menu, Skye scanned it to find something other than her regular turkey sandwich. "Have you had their tuna? Is it any good?"

"It's okay. It's tuna and mayonnaise. Hard to screw that up."

"I think I'm going to get the ham on rye."

"I'll call it in." Gwen picked up the phone. "Why the change today?"

"I always had turkey sandwiches with my dad."

"I'm just sticking my foot in it today, aren't I?"

Skye gave a nervous giggle. "You didn't know."

A waitress from the diner arrived with their sandwiches fifteen minutes later. Her umbrella did little to protect her from the rainstorm. The Styrofoam containers saved their sandwiches. "If you don't mind, I'm going to wait here until it slacks off some."

Gwen introduced Skye to Claire. "She and I go way back. How long has it been?"

"Ted and I moved here eight years ago, so eight years."

"We used to be neighbors."

Skye added, "So you know what it's like to be the new one in town."

"At least we're not alone. We have our husbands."

"I'm not married."

"Boyfriend?"

Skye shook her head.

Claire looked at Gwen. "Oh, I'm sorry. Wife...girlfriend?"

"None of the above," Skye giggled.

"We have to get you someone then. Who do you need to find you a love match, me or Gwen?"

"I don't understand."

Claire raised her hand to her mouth. "Oh, have you not told her?"

Gwen nodded. "She knows."

Skye's mouth opened. "I get it now. I guess I'd need you to find me someone, but I'm not looking right now. I'm still trying to get settled here."

"Well, when you're ready, you tell me. I have a gift for matchmaking. All but one of the couples I've set up have gotten married."

"I'll remember that," Skye smiled.

CHAPTER EIGHT

There was no sign of JJ's truck when Skye got home from work. But Sara was waiting for her. Skye couldn't definitely say Sara was watching for her, but she did come outside while Skye walked up the sidewalk to her house. She met her at the fence.

"I saw JJ was here."

"I took your suggestion and hired him to do the repair work for me."

"That's great. Do you like what he's done so far?"

"I don't know. I'm just getting home." Skye pointed to the house. "I haven't been inside to check yet."

"He's good. I'm sure you'll love him."

Skye waved and nodded. "I'm sure I will."

When she opened the front door, disappointment rained over her. She expected the house to be transformed, but she saw nothing but a note on the coffee table.

Skye,

> *I know it's tempting, but please don't touch any of the bricks in the fireplace. The cement isn't dry yet, and they could be moved out of place. I'll be back tomorrow.*

JJ

So Skye walked over to the fireplace and touched a brick. It didn't move, so she was satisfied that he had done a good job on it.

She kicked off her shoes and went into the kitchen to find something for dinner. "I should have picked up something." She opened and closed all the cabinets, even the ones with the glasses and plates. She opened the refrigerator. There sat three bottles of water. She pulled one out and looked at it. She knew it belonged to JJ, but she still couldn't resist the urge to hold it. Skye looked to see if he left any other treasures for her to find. There wasn't any, but she did see leftover Chinese food from the night before. "Looks like it's beef and peppers again tonight."

Skye put it in the microwave, container and all. While it heated, she poured herself a glass of Coke. She sat at the table and waited for her food to finish heating. She thought about eating at the table but decided sinking into the sofa, propping up her feet, and binge-watching something was the best idea.

Her laptop was hooked up to her television. She scrolled through her on demand options and found a RomCom to watch. Skye kicked backed and stared at her TV. Her mind drifted to JJ that morning. His grey eyes stood out more than the first time they met. She attributed it to the black tee he wore. When she thought about the jeans he wore, she wondered how he could breathe, let alone bend over in them. It wasn't a complaint. It was admiration. And it was high praise for his jeans and what filled them.

The fork entered her mouth empty. Skye looked into the container. At the bottom laid one piece of pepper. She stabbed it with her fork, then shoved it into her mouth. She stood up and carried the container and glass into the kitchen. The fork still in her mouth. She threw the empty food container into the trash walked to the sink, and as she set the glass in it, she opened her mouth and let the fork drop.

The clock struck nine. She looked at it like it lied to her. It was earlier than she normally showered but didn't want to stay up watching another movie. She could just rewatch the one that was just on. She knew it was about a girl who moved to New York and fell in love with a guy in her office, beyond that, she didn't know what she just watched. She did know she thought about JJ a lot that day.

The shower brought more than wet hair. She was wet all over the more she thought about JJ. Thinking about what was hiding under that tee and those jeans led to her imagining him joining her in the shower.

* * *

Skye was up, dressed, and waited for JJ arrive the next morning. She waited in her bedroom, so she didn't look like she was waiting for him. She stood far enough back from the front window, so she could still see her front gate but didn't look like she was watching for him.

The front of his truck pulled into view behind her car. He didn't get out right away. Every piece of her wanted to go outside to find out why. She fought herself and stayed put. Skye checked the clock – eight forty-three. She had time. *Who cares if I'm late? I own it and Gwen has a key.* Her heart pointed out that he was walking toward her gate. She saw him set down his toolbox and pick up Abby. Sara followed into the frame.

JJ tickled Abby's belly as he spoke with his sister. It looked to Skye that Sara was doing more talking. Eight forty-eight. She would have to leave now or be late. JJ set Abby down and picked up his toolbox. Skye ran downstairs. She opened the door as JJ reached the bottom step. He looked up at her.

His eyes were hidden behind sunglasses. "I hope you weren't waiting for me, so you could leave for work."

She grabbed the handrail and walked down slowly, the slit in her skirt revealing her thigh at each step. "No, I'm running late myself."

"Good."

Skye cocked her head to the side and lifted the left side of her mouth.

"I mean good you weren't waiting on me. Not good you're running late."

"Speaking of which, what should we do if I have to leave for work and you're not here?" If she were any closer to him, she would have been behind him. He smelled like a man. Skye wasn't sure what she meant when she thought it, but she knew it was accurate.

"You can leave the key with Sara."

"Nothing against your sister, but she sure can talk. Then I'd be late for work." She used her right hand to play with the fingers on her left hand.

"It's a safe town. You can leave your door unlock…"

Before he could finish, she chimed in, "No. I don't like to leave it unlocked when I'm not home."

JJ's surprised look told Skye no one had ever told him no about this before.

"I'll just lock the door and leave the key under the mat."

"That's the first place burglars look."

She sighed.

"How about on days when I know I'll be late, I'll call you and pick up the key at your store?"

"That's a great idea." She reached into her purse and looked at her phone. Three minutes after nine. "Speaking of the store, I have to go. It's after nine. I'm officially late." She started to walk away. "Bye." She waved to him over her shoulder.

"Wait," he called after her. She turned around. "Is the door unlocked?"

"Yes. I saw you coming up the walk and didn't lock it."

Skye went off to work for the second day with a JJ smile on her face.

CHAPTER NINE

Skye ran out of excuses. After two weeks of saying, "I can't. I have plans," in response to Gwen's invitation to join her and Quinn for dinner, she agreed. Skye hadn't had barbeque chicken on the grill in years, and Gwen's invitation enticed her.

The thought of being found out lived in the front of Skye's mind. She was grateful it let her rest at work, after a month of her heart pounding every time the bell on the door jingled when anyone entered. But being at someone's house, having to carry on conversations, and not being able to escape by having Gwen take care of the customer, sent panic streaming throughout her body.

I should have said no or backed out. She knocked on the door. A man answered.

"I'm sorry. I must have the wrong address."

"Are you looking for Gwen or Quinn?"

The man could tell Skye nodded yes only because he was looking at her head.

"You've got the right address. Come on in." Skye stepped inside, carrying a bowl covered in aluminum foil. "They're in the kitchen."

Skye gave the minimal nod again. She walked through the living room and dining room into the kitchen, followed by the man who let her in.

"Hey, you made it," Gwen said.

"Yeah." Skye looked at all the eyes that were focused on her. She avoided eye contact. Grammy always said the eyes were the pathway to the soul. By looking someone in the eye, you could tell if they were telling the truth or not. If she didn't look anyone in the eye, they couldn't see she was a fraud. "I brought this." She handed the bowl to Gwen.

"You didn't have to bring anything." Gwen lifted the foil. "What is it?"

"My grandmother always said you should bring something when you're invited to someone's house. So I made her Cherry Surprise. It's like a parfait all mixed together."

"It looks yummy. Thank you. Let me introduce you."

Gwen went in a circle, introducing everyone in the room. Each one made some movement in response to their name. "That's Rick. Behind him is Bart. You know Claire. That's Maria. Her husband, Brooks. Beside him is Quinn. And you met Ted at the door."

Great, I'm the fifth wheel.

"This is my boss, Skye."

She lifted her hand and lowered her head to say hello.

Claire rushed around the counter. "I knew you needed me to introduce you to someone."

Brooks chimed in. "Don't start on her already, Claire. It's because of you, I'm stuck with her." He pointed at Maria as though he were hitchhiking, as she slapped his shoulder.

"So, I just need you to tell me a few things about yourself, and I'll find Mr. Right for you."

Skye used her right hand to play with the fingers on her left hand. She didn't want to answer any questions about herself. One wrong word and her secret would be out in the open.

"Dark hair or light?"

Quinn stepped in to save her from Claire, even though her question wasn't much better. "Skye, you moved into the old Vandermeer place, didn't you?"

"Yes, I did."

"I heard the mother kept the daughter's room intact. Was it still a kid's room when you bought it?"

"It still is."

Everyone in the room stopped and looked at Skye. Sweat formed and ran down her back.

Brooks jumped in. "No way. You're keeping the kiddy shrine?"

Skye's breathing quickened.

"Isn't it creepy sleeping in a house with a dead kid's stuff?"

"Shut up, Bart," Quinn ordered.

"What? The kid's been gone for twenty years. She's got to be dead."

Skye pressed her tongue to the roof of her mouth to keep from crying. *She's not dead. She's right here.* The thought was so loud in her head, she was surprised everyone in the room couldn't hear it.

Gwen asked, "Want something to drink?"

"Yes, please."

Bart continued, "Can we see it?"

Quinn pointed to Bart. "Chill out."

Gwen handed Skye a glass of white wine. "Dinner's ready. Let's go outside."

As though they had been assigned a dish, everyone picked up one and headed out the back door. Skye asked Quinn, "Is there anything I can help with?"

Quinn handed her a basket with rolls. "Thank you."

While everyone enjoyed dinner and good conversation, Skye listened more than she spoke. Whenever she looked at Bart, he was looking at her. Her heart would speed up each time. But not the way it sped up when she saw or thought about JJ. His eyes burned her. It was as though he had the ability to see inside her and knew she was lying about something. Her awkward smiles were returned with raised eyebrows. Bart was the car wreck her eyes had to pass because he sat across from her. She tried to avoid looking at him, but there was a morbid curiosity filling her. *Stop staring at me.* Skye wondered what she had said to clue in Bart to who she was.

The conversation continued even when the food ended. Skye learned Ted was a firefighter which led her thoughts to JJ. She wondered what he was doing then. She hoped he was visiting Sara. Then she could borrow something or ask for help with something, so she could get a peek at him. She smiled to herself, *I could always sit on the porch or watch out the front window until he left.* Each time her thoughts landed on him, he was wearing the black tee, jeans, and work boots. Even when she thought about the night they met, her mind dressed him to be ready for work.

Everyone helped clear the table. Bart stopped Skye when she came out to retrieve more from the table. "I'm sorry for my comments earlier."

"You're fine."

"Rose was my cousin. Everyone, except my Aunt Alice, believes her father killed her. Most of us think he killed himself, too. I've gotten a little jaded about the whole thing."

"A little jaded?" She looked at his mouth, so he couldn't look into her eyes.

"It's all I've heard about my whole life."

A delayed reaction hit her. *Oh my God! You're my cousin.* She looked at his face to see if they shared any features. She wanted to find something, anything that said they were related. Her eyes darted from his eyes to his mouth, to his nose, to his forehead, even his ears.

"Are you okay?" he asked.

What did I do? "Yes, why do you ask?"

"Your eyes looked like they were about to roll back into your head."

"I guess the wine just hit me."

"Didn't you only have two glasses?"

She shrugged. "Yeah, I guess I'm kind of a lightweight when it comes to drinking." Once again, she scanned his face, but slower this time so he didn't think she was about to pass out.

* * *

Her mind fought itself to think about two different men during her drive home. One turned her on, and one could be the first blood relative she's met in twenty years. Skye looked for JJ's truck when she pulled up at home. "He'd be driving his car since he's not working," she reminded herself. Neither was parked at Sara's house.

She made her way into her house. A volleyball game of thoughts played in her head. "JJ walked here...Bart's probably been here...JJ has a great smile...Bart's seen my mother smile." *Stop it! Stop thinking about Bart. You don't know if he's your cousin.*

Skye went straight to her room and changed for bed. She didn't worry about brushing her teeth. She climbed under the covers and turned out the light. The dark that took over her room only brightened her thoughts. The recorder in her head replayed Bart's words, "Rose was my cousin. Everyone, except my Aunt Alice, believes her father killed her."

"He didn't. He protected me."

"Most of us think he killed himself, too."

"He didn't. He died three months ago."

It was on repeat until she escaped into the dream world that included JJ holding her.

CHAPTER TEN

The door had been closed the day Skye moved in and remained that way. Today was the day it would change. At least that was Skye's intent. She stared at the door, like a punished child who had been told to stand in the corner. If she had been asleep, it would be considered sleep paralysis. But she was awake and terrified.

There were toys on the other side of the door that had not been played with in twenty years. There was a bed that no one had snuggled under the covers to keep warm for two decades. There were clothes for a little girl to play in and dress up in. All on the other side of the door. On Skye's side of the door, there was a young woman who may have been the little girl who did those things.

The doorknob turned with ease, but her body was stiff. Her legs were heavy. They refused to listen when she told them to walk into the room. There was no need for her to be afraid of what lay before her, but Bart's words rang in her ears, "Everyone, except my Aunt Alice, believes her father killed her." Skye hoped that there was something, anything that would spark a memory, or at least a familiar feeling, which would make her know she was on the right track. The heaviness in her soul over the loss of her father had ripped open a hole in heart – a hole that she filled in years before to cover the pain of being a teenage girl without a mother.

She sat on the floor in the hallway, looking into the childless room filled with toys. Something Skye never considered before crossed her mind. "What if my father was Connor Vandermeer and he killed Rose and I'm someone else?" She refused to entertain that thought ever again.

Her father always told her that he'd do anything for her.

"Daddy, what would you do if someone tried to kidnap me?" a young Skye asked one afternoon at the park.

"I'd run after them. Then I'd punch him in the nose." He jumped off the swing he was on beside her. "Then I'd pull each hair out of his head." He pulled some grass as an example.

"What if he's bald?" she asked.

"Then I'd yank his nose until it was as big as Pinocchio's."

Skye giggled.

Her father smiled and hugged her. "You're my world and I'll always do everything I can to make sure you're always right here beside me."

Skye's thoughts returned to the present. "Nah, I'm either really Skye Maxwell or Rose Vandermeer. Whoever I am, I'm cleaning out that room today."

She stepped into the room and looked around more thoroughly than she did the day she put the offer on the house. She did all she could that day to not draw attention to herself. Skye laughed at the thought. "I didn't want to be suspicious, so I offered $5,000 more. Yeah, I'm a brainiac."

A doll sat in the corner on a child-size rocking chair. Skye walked over, picked it up, and held it to her chest. She hoped for a connection, a memory, anything that let her remember this doll. But there was nothing.

A strange thought crossed her mind. She kneeled on the floor, still clutching the doll. A three-year-old is only this tall. Maybe if I'm at the same height, the view would remind me. She traced the room once again, taking her time attempting to force a memory, but all she saw was the room before her.

She retrieved a cardboard box which hadn't been assembled yet from the pile in the hall. She carried it into the bedroom and taped it together. Opening the first drawer, she looked at piles of neatly folded shirts. She pulled one out and let it unfold as she lifted it; a green shirt with puppies. "Cute." She refolded it, then put it in the box. She repeated it for every shirt, although she changed the adjective to describe the shirt in her hand. After the last one, she closed the box and then taped it shut. With the magic marker she had in her back pocket, she wrote SHIRTS on the top.

As Skye progressed to the next drawer, she didn't pick up each one individually. Instead, she grabbed a pile. Any connection she hoped to feel or find was not in the dresser full of clothes. She emptied each drawer, marking each box as she filled it.

Opening the closet door, she saw it was stocked with frilly dresses. She pulled one out and looked at it. She decided it was too pretty to fold, so she removed the hanger and laid it flat in the box. Each one was given the same treatment. When Skye removed a pink dress with lace at the bottom, a memory flashed in her head – a toddler in a dress like this one sitting on the Easter Bunny's lap. She closed her eyes and tried to remember more, but all she could see was a snapshot in her mind's eye of a girl and the Easter Bunny. She opened her eyes. Skye wondered if she remembered her time as Rose or if her father had dressed her in a similar dress. She finished removing the dresses from the closet.

The next thing she tackled was the pile of stuffed animals. Having given up on finding anything that brought back a memory, Skye sat on the floor next to them and dropped them into the box.

Skye felt proud of getting the room boxed. A feeling of sadness fought for her attention, but she refused to let it win. She knew finding out if she was Rose was going to be hard, especially with keeping it quiet. Therefore little victories such as this would have to get her through to the truth. She did admit to herself that the bed looked sad without any bedding on it.

A thought crossed her mind as Skye surveyed the results of her hard work. She had no way of getting all of the boxes to the thrift store. She would need someone with a truck, so all the boxes, dresser, and bed would fit. Because she didn't know many people in town, it was a short list: Sara? No. Tyler? No. Gwen? Her car barely fit her. The thought that should have been first came to mind – JJ.

Skye grabbed her phone from on top of the dresser, searched her contacts, and called him.

"Hello."

"Hi, JJ. It's Skye."

"I know."

"I was wondering if you were busy today. I am cleaning out the room that belonged to the little girl who lived here and need someone who has a truck to help me get the stuff to the thrift store." Then she added, "I'll pay you."

"I'd love to help, but I'm working."

"When you get off?"

"I'm at the firehouse. I don't get off until eight tomorrow morning."

"Would you be available tomorrow?"

"Sure. About two?"

"That'll be great. Thank you."

After hanging up, she looked around the room once again. Skye had nothing else planned that day. She decided to take apart the bed. "This way everything will be ready to go tomorrow."

Skye moved the boxes against the wall to have space to put the mattress and box spring. She held the handles and pulled the mattress off onto the floor. It landed with a dull thud. On the box spring laid a book. She picked it up. It was a journal. *Rose was too young to write, so this must be her mother's.* Skye wondered if she should read it or not. Her curiosity won.

Laying across the mattress, she opened to the first page and read:

Today marks four years since my precious Rose disappeared. People have stopped calling to check on me, but the pain remains...

Page after page recounted Rose's mother's days without her daughter; the things she wished she could be doing with her. Guilt overtook Skye when she read parts when the girl's mother would plead for Rose to find a phone and call her, but her interest kept her reading.

One passage caught her attention and held it.

Dear Rose,

I know you can't read this, but I feel as though it's the only connection we still have. Last night, Robert Alderman asked me to marry him. We've been dating for two years now. I worried that if I married him and changed my last name, you would never be able to find me. Today Robert gave me an ultimatum – marry him or break up with him. I chose break up with him. He wanted me to be Alice Alderman. I couldn't give up any of the ways left for you to find me.

She read it multiple times. Rose's mother last name was still Vandermeer, at least it was sixteen years ago. However, a moment later she realized she already knew this. When she bought the house, she knew the seller's name was Alice Vandermeer. At least she knew why Rose's mother never changed her name.

It was dark outside by the time Skye finished reading Alice Vandermeer's private words. She closed the book and ran her hand over the cover. "I think I'm home, Mom." She smiled at the thought of having a mother after all of these years.

* * *

JJ arrived a little after two the next day.

"You're late," Skye smiled.

He pointed next door, "I was being held captive by a three-foot-tall monster."

I'd like to hold you captive. "How'd you escape?"

"It's naptime."

"Everything is upstairs, but ready to go." Skye turned and headed up the steps.

JJ stood there for a moment. Skye's shorts didn't reveal everything, but there was a clear view high up the inside of her thigh.

"You coming?"

"Almost." He jogged up the steps behind her.

They started with the bed. JJ volunteered to be the one who went down the steps backward. "Let me lead so you don't push me down them." These seemed like reasonable directions until JJ hollered, "Slow down. You're going to kill me. I'm going down backwards."

"Sorry."

Skye didn't attempt to kill him when they carried the dresser.

For every box Skye carried to the truck, JJ carried two. She saw sweat roll down the side of his face as he lifted the last box into the bed of his pick-up.

"Can I get you something to drink?"

"Sounds good."

They sat on the top step of her porch drinking bottled water. JJ took a swig, then asked, "What are you going to do with the room now?"

Skye shrugged. "I'm not sure. I have two things in mind."

"They are?"

"I like to paint. I'm not any good, but I like to do it. Or get a treadmill and a rowing machine, so maybe I'll work out more."

"So, you want a room where you go in, can't decide what you want to paint, then go watch TV or a room to have extra space to hang stuff."

Skye laughed. "Yes, exactly."

JJ handed her the empty water bottle and said, "Well, I'd better get this stuff over there before they close."

"Do you want me to follow you?"

"You don't have to go. They have people there to help unload."

"Then let me get my checkbook."

"For what?"

"I said I'd pay you for this."

"If you were selling the stuff, I'd accept it. But you're donating it. It would be wrong for me to take money for driving it there."

"But..."

"I won't cash it if you give it to me."

"Thank you."

Skye didn't stand up. She had box seats to watch JJ walk away. *I could watch him walk away all day.* He looked at her before getting into the truck. She waved. He lifted his hand in response. Watching him drive away was not as satisfying as watching him walk away.

CHAPTER ELEVEN

Skye could hear JJ hammering. She had hoped to sleep in, after being up late the previous night watching videos online. "I'm never doing this again," always turned into, "One more," and she paid for it the next morning. "I might as well get up and do the yardwork I wanted to get done." She kicked off the sheet and crawled out of bed.

The hammering echoed under the half-finished deck. Skye looked up and squinted into the early morning sun, shielding her eyes to see JJ at the top of the ladder. Blue jeans that highlighted his ass and no shirt. *At least give me a fighting chance.* His tool belt pulled his jeans down on one side enough for her to tell he wears tighty whities – in a light shade of blue.

"Good morning," she called up to him.

"Jesus Christ. You scared the hell out of me. You shouldn't startle someone who's on a ladder."

"I'm sorry. I just wanted to say hello."

"Hello."

"Is it safe for me to walk under to get the hose?"

"Yeah, it's safe." Skye could see JJ watching as she walked in the shade of the deck. She emphasized her hips sway left and right with each step she took. Shorts, not much larger than bikini bottoms, and the top to a swimsuit. Her hair pulled into a messy bun.

Skye pulled the hose to the garden she had planted the week before. The rose bushes looked to have some growth. The daffodils were looking healthy, but there was no sign of the marigolds. Being so late in the growing season, she didn't expect much from either, but she couldn't help but hope.

JJ yelled, "Shit!"

His yell startled Skye. She turned in time to see him hit the ground and the ladder come down on top of him. He brought his arms up to protect his face before it hit him.

"Oh my God. Are you okay?" she called as she ran to him.

He pushed the ladder off him. "Yeah, just embarrassed." He sat up.

"Are you hurt?"

JJ looked at the marks on his arms where the rungs and side of the ladder hit him. "No, just a bruised ego."

Skye stood up and put her hands on her hips. "Aren't you a firefighter?"

He nodded.

"Didn't they teach you to use one of these things?"

"Yes, they did." He stood up.

She gestured a turning motion as she told him to turn around.

He turned and looked at her over his shoulder. "What?"

Wiping the grass that stuck to his back, she said, "Just getting this off you. How'd it happen?"

"I was paying attention to something else, instead of what I was doing. I missed a rung and pulled the ladder down on top of myself." JJ lifted the ladder back into position.

"Why don't you come inside and rest for a little bit?"

"No, I'm fine. I only fell from the bottom rung. My ego is bruised," he looked at his right arm, "and my arm, but I'm okay."

Skye watched him climb the ladder again. She watched his butt climb the ladder, the rest of him happened to be attached to it.

When he was at the top, he reached for his hammer, then climbed back down the ladder.

"Be careful. There's a rung right here." She pointed to the one at the bottom.

"Oh ha ha," he replied as he jumped off the ladder, avoiding the last rung altogether. He walked to his toolbox and grabbed a box of nails. He emptied it into a pocket of his tool belt. JJ smiled when he turned around and saw Skye watching him.

"You don't have to watch me. I'm fine."

Oh yes, you are fine. "I'm just making sure. You fell on my property. I don't want you to sue me." *That was stupid. He must think I'm horrible now and don't care about him.*

"I'm okay, and I'm not going to sue you. It was my fault."

"I didn't mean that. I meant…"

He smiled again. "I know what you meant. It's okay."

* * *

JJ would descend the ladder, move it, climb back up and hammer more. This went on for an hour. Skye would call to him to be careful a few times he came down. He'd reply with a "ha ha" or a sarcastic "Thanks." Meanwhile, she found reasons to stay in the backyard for as long as possible. Sara and Abby coming outside helped her remain outside.

Abby ran to the fence. "Unca JJ." She waved.

"Hey Princess," he called back.

"Careful. It's further to the ground from there," Skye joked as she walked to the fence to speak to Sara.

"You're funny."

Sara's eyes darted between Skye and JJ. "What's that about?"

Skye tried to hold back a laugh but wasn't successful. "Your brother, the fireman, fell off the ladder earlier today."

"Oh my God. He fell off the ladder, and you're making a joke about it." Sara climbed over the fence. She turned to Abby, "Wait right here."

"'kay."

Skye tried to stop her. "No it's okay. He and I have joked about it already. He's fine." She hopped alongside Sara. "I'm not like that. I wouldn't make fun of someone who was hurt."

When the pair reached the bottom of the ladder, Sara called up to him, "Are you okay?"

"Yeah, I'm fine. Why?"

"Skye told me you fell off the ladder."

As he came down the ladder, Skye reiterated. "He's okay. I asked him a couple of times."

"I'm fine."

"Are you sure? Should you go to the ER be checked?"

"Sara, you have to listen. I. Am. Alright. I fell from here." He pointed to the lowest rung. He looked at Skye. "See what happens when you tell momma bird what happened?" JJ turned back to Sara. "Stop worrying about me. I'm a grown man. And you're my little sister. I'm supposed to take care of you."

"But you don't have anyone to take care of you."

"Let's not get into this now. I have a deck to finish."

Abby screamed.

The three adults turned and saw her lying on the ground on Skye's side of the fence. All three ran in her direction.

JJ arrived first and was kneeling beside her before either of the girls got to Abby. Sara reached to pick her up. JJ stopped her.

"Don't move her." He turned his attention back to Abby. "Did you hit your head?"

She nodded as she cried.

"Does it hurt when you breathe?"

She shook her head no.

"What hurts?"

Abby pointed to the back of her head.

Skye watched as he examined his niece. JJ continued to ask Abby questions about her fall. He determined she didn't land on her head. He asked her questions about her favorite doll. When he concluded that she didn't have a major injury, he picked her up and then stood up.

"Are you okay now, Princess?" he asked.

She nodded again.

"She seems to be okay. But if I were you, I'd take her to the ER just to be safe. She fell from something that's the same height as her."

"Thank you. I'll take her right away." Sara climbed over the fence. JJ handed Abby to her.

Skye and JJ watched Sara carry Abby into the house. Skye would glance at JJ's bare chest but kept most of her focus on Sara and Abby.

"That was scary," Skye said after Sara disappeared into her house.

"Eh."

"What do you mean 'eh'? I'm still shaking."

"It's my job. I do it all the time." He showed no emotion as he walked away.

Skye was not interested in watching his ass this time as he walked away. She was more confused by how cold he acted. She jogged to catch him before he ascended the ladder again. She touched his arm. He turned to her.

"But that was your niece."

JJ's head jerked up and down.

"And it was just another day for you?"

"I was more than aware that it was my niece. But all my years of experience and training kick in when something like that happens. If I hadn't been able to separate my emotions from what was going on, she could be paralyzed now if she had landed on the top of her head. Now, which would you prefer? The emotionless me or the one who made it so my niece could never walk again?"

Skye looked at the ground. "I hadn't thought about that."

JJ walked to his toolbox.

"I'm sorry." She followed him. "I've never experienced anything like that before. That's the first time I have ever seen anything like that. The most I've seen was my friend's skinning a knee or my dad cutting his finger when he was making dinner. And both only needed a band-aid."

"I guess it could seem cold-hearted to anyone who hadn't experienced it before."

Skye smiled.

"But you can guarantee I'll be on the phone later making sure Abby's fine, if they're not back before I leave."

She smiled wider.

JJ followed the hose from the wall to the nozzle. He picked it up and took a drink.

"Ew, I can't believe you drank out of that. There's glasses and fresh water in the house."

"It's the same water that's in the house."

"But it's the hose."

He flicked his wrist in her direction, leaving a trail of water. "It's water. It won't hurt you. And I didn't dirty one of your glasses this way."

"You still have bottles of water in my fridge."

"That, too." He smiled and handed the hose to Skye.

Damn! Sunlight reflected in his eyes.

JJ turned to walk away and turned back when the cold water hit his back. Skye pointed the hose to the ground.

"What?" she said with a smile. "It's water. It won't hurt you."

"You did not just squirt me with the hose."

Skye shrugged. "Would I do that?"

He walked toward her. "Yes, you would."

Skye lifted the hose and let the spray shower JJ. She squealed when he got to her and wrestled the hose from her. JJ grabbed her and spun her around, pulling her to him. He held her in front of him with his left arm, while he sprayed her, while she laughed.

JJ let go of her as fast as he grabbed her. "I'd better get back to this if I'm going finish this today." He put both hands in his front pockets and walked away.

CHAPTER TWELVE

Skye walked through her repaired house. Everything JJ had promised to do was done and exceeded her expectations. It was her house now. At least it looked like it. She still didn't feel like it was.

Sitting on the floor of the empty room which once belonged to Rose, Skye compared her life to the room. "There once was a toddler whose life was perfect. Then her father threw a wrench in it and wreaked havoc. And now the room is empty, looking for what it will be next."

It forced her to examine her life. She lied on the floor with her fingers interlaced on the top of her head. "What if I'm not Rose? What if I am just Skye Maxwell from Malibu, California? Dad was so heavily medicated that he may have just remembered hearing about it and thought it was true."

She sat up. "I shouldn't have bought this house. Now I'm stuck here no matter what."

Skye ran her fingers through her hair then brought her hands to her face. "Then I went and bought a business and spent the rest of the money repairing this place. I've built a prison for myself and threw away the key."

She stomped her feet. "Eh," she yelled. "What was I thinking going off half-cocked like that? Dad always told me to think before I did. But no - I had to do, then think."

She thought about contacting her grandparents and telling them where she was and why. But she couldn't do that to her father. She was positive they didn't know the secret. Telling them would create a new problem that she didn't have the energy to deal with.

Her thoughts trailed back to something she thought earlier. "How would my father know about the kidnapping if he didn't do it unless he'd been here before?" She sat up. "Oh my God! That's it!" Skye grabbed her shoes and purse and ran out to her car.

* * *

Skye pulled up to the high school. She walked in, straight and tall, scared to death. She eyed the line of five individual doors. She started in the middle and pulled on the handle, but it didn't budge. The door to the right of it opened with ease.

What am I doing? I can't just ask. She moved down the hallway. Skye looked in the doors of the unoccupied classrooms until she found the office. She stood staring at the door, wondering if she should knock or just enter. She reached for the doorknob and flung it open, startling a lady at a desk behind a counter.

"May I help you?"

Skye took a deep breath. "I don't know who I need to speak with."

The lady walked to the counter in time with Skye. "Tell me what you need, and I'll direct you to the right person."

Skye used her right hand to play with the fingers on her left hand. "I was wondering if it was possible for me to look at some old yearbooks."

"What year did you graduate?"

"I didn't go here."

"Then I'm sorry. We only allow current and former students to view the yearbooks. There's a lot of crazies out there, you know."

I should have lied. "My mother graduated from here."

"Oh, okay. And what year did she graduate?"

Skye pulled on one of her fingernails on her left hand. "The truth is, I'm adopted. I'm trying to find my birth mother. I know she graduated from Centerville High, but I don't know which one." Skye was never good at thinking up lies on the spot, but she impressed herself this time.

"There's only one high school here, so you must have the right one. Wait here a minute. I'll get Mr. Campbell to help you.

Skye meant that there was more than one Centerville High in the U.S., not in the town. But her lie got her one step closer to searching yearbooks for her father's picture. She moved around the office, looking at the pictures on the wall.

Skye turned around when she said heard a man say hello.

She walked back to the counter. "Hi."

The man extended his hand to her. As she reached for it, he said, "I'm Jerry Campbell. Miss Payne told me you'd like to look through some old yearbooks in an attempt to find your birth mother."

Skye nodded.

"What year did she graduate?"

"I don't know."

"What was her name?"

"I don't know." *Yeah, this is going to be me thrown out instead of looking at the yearbooks.*

He turned his head to the side but kept his eyes on Skye. "If you don't have that information, I don't know how I can help you."

"I know approximately what year she graduated. But I've been given a few variations of her name." She resumed playing with the fingers on her left hand. "I don't know if it's a nickname and her real name or what."

Mr. Campbell thought for a moment. He told Skye to sign-in and had her follow him down the hall to the library. "They're all right here." He pointed to a three-shelf bookcase underneath a horse painted on the wall, the school's mascot. "Please stop by the office and sign-out when you're done or if you need any help."

"I will."

"I hope you find what you're looking for."

"Thank you."

Skye stooped down to read the years on the books as Mr. Campbell returned to his office. She pulled out three books, placed them on the table. She opened the first one. Page-by-page she examined every face to see if any looked like her father. When she got to each class' individual pictures, she checked for William Maxwell and Connor Vandermeer. She didn't find a picture with either name or who looked like him. She did this for each one.

Wait. What if Daddy lied about his age? She did the math in her head. *Connor Vandermeer would be 46, which means he would have graduated twenty-two years ago. Daddy was 50.* She wondered if she had found proof he hadn't kidnapped her or if he lied about his age to hide his identity. She put the three books back.

Skye had started with the wrong year and was going in the wrong direction. She pulled out three more. She flipped to the Senior portraits – no Connor Vandermeer or William Maxwell.

She searched but didn't find him. But she found Alice Rasmussen's senior portrait. Being the only Alice, she deduced that this was Rose's mother. She studied the picture, then looked at her reflection in the window. Everyone always said she looked like her father. She had hoped for anything that looked similar, but there was none.

She returned the books, signed out, then drove home. She sat with her face in her hands. She was still without any proof of who she really was.

CHAPTER THIRTEEN

Restful was the last word Skye would use to describe the
previous night's sleep. It was bad enough that the smoke
detector went off in the middle of the night, but she
couldn't get back to sleep after she returned to bed.

Her childhood wasn't a Norman Rockwell painting.
She believed there should be a mom and dad for that. But
her father made it as perfect as any childhood could be. She
never gave any thought to Grammy and Poppy not being
her real grandparents until she was alone in the dark.

How could her father give her life-shattering
information when he was in no condition to answer her
questions? Why didn't he tell her sooner or even tell her at
all? She knew the answer to that one – he wanted to clear
his conscience before he died and didn't want to be arrested
for telling her sooner, if it was true. Skye closed her eyes as
her mind was hijacked by the memory of her father's
confession.

*Skye held her father's hand and watched his chest
rise and fall, thankful each time it rose. He sighed. His eyes
fluttered as he fought to awaken from another morphine-
induced nap. "Skye?"*

*She jumped from her seat to make it easier for him
to see her. "I'm here, Daddy."*

*"Skye, I have to tell you something." His eyes
darkened. His voice cracked. There was a tone which told
her he was not going to just say he loves her yet again.
"Skye...Baby Girl...I lied to you."*

"It's okay, Daddy."

He gripped her hand tighter. "No, it's not okay. My lie ruined your life."

Skye pushed her lower lip up until her upper lip touched her nose, her confused look. "Daddy, my life wasn't ruined. You made it great." She cupped his hand between hers. His colorless face became transparent. Tears rolled down the side of his face. Panic raced through her bloodstream.

"I destroyed your life, and you don't even know it." His eyes grabbed hers and didn't let go. "I'm not Bill Maxwell."

Knowing her father had been saying some strange things because of being medicated to the point of confusion, she let out a snicker. "Daddy."

"It's true. And you're not Skye Maxwell." She cocked her head to the side. "I brought you out here without anyone knowing."

"Daddy, what are you saying?"

He took a deep breath. His grip loosened. "I kidnapped you."

"No." Her response was not one of disbelief, but one of non-acceptance.

"It's true, Skye. I kidnapped you."

Skye shook her head. She couldn't believe what he said. His words used her ear canal as an echo chamber. As they reached her brain, she muttered, "You're not...I mean...Who...Umm..." She forced herself to ask the question, "Do you know who my parents are?"

"I'm your father."

Skye relaxed. It's just the drugs talking. She smiled, "Okay Daddy."

He continued, "I took you from your mother when you were three. She wasn't going to let me see you anymore." His words were more coherent than any he had uttered the past two weeks. "I couldn't live without you, Rose."

Wrong name. He's delirious. "Well, I'm glad you did it, Daddy. I would have missed you."

The beeps on his heart monitor increased. "Your real name is Rose, Rose Vandermeer from Centerville."

A nurse rushed in. And the another who made her leave her father's room.

Skye had never broached the subject again.

CHAPTER FOURTEEN

Skye paused the movie before answering the ringing phone. "Hello."

"Hi. It's JJ."

Skye smiled as she repeated her greeting.

"I've got some bad news for you."

Her mind raced, trying to figure out what type of bad news he might have for her.

"I have your bill ready."

"Oh," she laughed.

"Do you mind if I drop it off later? I'm going over Sara's tonight."

"I don't mind. I'll be home all evening."

"I'll see you this evening then."

Skye didn't notice the smile she was wearing as she hung up the phone.

* * *

Skye bound to the door in a Pavlovian response to the knock. Knowing JJ would be on the other side of the door quickened her step. She saw him waving next door as he waited on her porch. She could tell by his wave that Abby was waving to him. He jumped when she opened the door.

"Hey," JJ smiled.

"Hi," not hiding her smile as she opened the door wider. "Come on in."

JJ handed an envelope to her as he entered.

She opened it and peaked at the paper inside without removing it from its paper cave. "Oh."

"Well, that's not good."

"No, that was a good oh. I was expecting it to be higher."

"Gimme a pen, and I can fix that for you."

"It's okay. I can suffer enough with this one. When do you need the money?"

JJ shrugged. "No rush. Whenever you can."

Skye replied, "I misplaced my checkbook. I'll get it to you in a day or two."

"That's fine."

They stood, staring at each other. She could see whiskers peeking from his jaw, just enough to tell her he had shaved that morning. She wrestled with the desire to feel his growing beard on her cheek.

Skye heard the silence crumble away when JJ spoke. "Well, I should get over there before they wonder what happened to me." He pointed over his shoulder with his thumb. "Abby saw me come in here."

"Don't let me hold you up." *Just let me hold you.* "I'll get this to you tomorrow." She lifted the hand that held the envelope.

"No rush. I know where you live." His smile was like a defibrillator to her chest. Skye could feel the shock from it jumpstart her heart. It pounded in her ears. She used her right hand to play with the fingers on her left hand, which still held the envelope. JJ reached for the doorknob as he turned to leave. "Time to go be Uncle JJ."

"Have fun." She waved the envelope, not caring how silly it looked.

* * *

Skye called JJ from work the next day. "I found my checkbook. I left it at work. Whenever you want to come by, I'll have your check for you."

"I'm a few blocks from your house now, doing some work. I can stop by when I finish here if that's okay."

"That'll be fine."

As she pressed the disconnect button, Skye asked Gwen, "Are you supposed to tip a handyman?"

"Of course. And don't forget to write a check to tip me, too."

"Seriously. Do I tip him?"

"No, you're paying him to do a job, just like you pay me. However, I'm pretty sure we both need a raise."

Skye's face lit up with her laugh.

* * *

The pair stood as they had the previous night. Skye tried to find a reason why JJ should stay longer than just picking up a check.

"Here you go." Skye had to look at his hand reaching for the check. His gaze was too intense. It was like staring into the sun, but the gaze did not burn her eyes. It branded her deep in her chest. She knew if anyone could see her heart, the letters JJ would be there.

"Thanks…and thanks for getting it to me so quickly. Most people make me wait until I call and remind them three or four times."

"I'm not most people." *I didn't just say that.*

"I noticed." His burning gaze moved to his smile. The heat which branded her heart transformed to electricity dancing in her stomach.

The silence they had shared the previous night had returned. But the awkwardness kept its distance. He was content to be in her presence. She was happy experiencing the gamut of emotions he stirred in her. When their eyes met, they locked into place until one got the strength to look away. It wasn't a startled looking away, but rather moving the stare to the others nose or mouth. His jawline wasn't darkened by whiskers, but still called for her attention.

"Since I'm no longer working for you, I was wondering something."

Skye didn't reply, but instead bobbed her head three times. She used her left hand to play with the fingers on her right hand while he spoke.

"Would you want to, maybe, go to dinner with me sometime?"

Time stopped for Skye. Time sped up. Time was not a measurement for her. Instead, it was tangible, holding her in place, while it pushed her into the unknown. An unknown she couldn't wait to explore. She replied with an awkward smile, "I'd love to."

"Great. How about tomorrow? Say about six?"

"That's perfect. How about I make us dinner here?"

"I thought we could go somewhere."

"I want to. I like to cook." She couldn't understand why she was comfortable at the store, but not being out in public. There was an unrealistic feeling of safety she had created in her store that didn't carry over to anyplace else in town.

"If we stay here, Sara will probably be here the entire time."

"Where did you say we're going?"

"I'll see you tomorrow at six?"

Skye agreed.

JJ walked out the door sideways, keeping eye contact with Skye. His hand dragged along the door behind him as it opened wider. "I'll see you tomorrow."

The smile they shared grew wider on Skye's face. No words escaped her as she nodded in agreement.

CHAPTER FIFTEEN

JJ arrived five minutes late, but Skye didn't hold it against him. Seeing him in a raspberry red dress shirt and jeans made her want to hold him against her. "Sorry I'm late. Sara was leaving as I pulled up, so I had to pretend I was going there."

"Don't you think you should get to know me a little better before you're embarrassed to tell your sister we're going out?"

"Trust me, it's better if she doesn't know yet. She'll drive us both crazy wanting to know all about it and trying to get us married."

"Married? How about we actually go somewhere before we talk about marriage?" Skye grabbed her purse.

"Sara has been trying to get me married to someone for almost ten years. She and Ty have been together since high school. So, she believes I should be happily married now, too. Ready?"

"Ready." They walked out onto the porch. Skye turned and double checked to make sure the door was locked. Their conversation continued as they walked to his car. "So, they got married right out of high school?"

"Like a year after. Ty went away to college for a year. They got married that summer. Then he transferred to college here. And ever since then, it's been Sara's mission to get me married off." JJ opened Skye's door. After she was in, he walked around and got in, closing the door and sliding the key into the ignition in one motion.

"I'm confused. They haven't been married ten years, have they?"

"Originally, her goal was to find me a girlfriend. Once she was married, she decided big brother should be married, too. So together it's been a total of about ten years. Do you like seafood?"

"I love seafood. If you don't mind me asking, how much older are you?" She sat sideways, watching JJ as he spoke.

"Four years, I'm twenty-eight."

"Hmm." She turned forward.

JJ looked at her longer than someone who's driving should take their eyes off the road. When he looked back at the road ahead, he asked, "Is that a bad thing?"

Skye's cheeks matched the red light, they were approaching. "No, not at all. I thought you two were closer in age."

JJ responded with a nod of his head.

The rest of the drive passed in silence.

* * *

There was a short wait for a table. When the hostess asked if they wanted to wait in the bar, Skye shrugged, so JJ told her no. The silence between them echoed loudly in Skye's ears. *Say something, Stupid.* She opened her mouth as the hostess directed them to follow her.

"Is this okay?"

Skye smiled. JJ replied, "Yes, thank you."

The hostess handed them each a menu. "Can I get you anything to drink?"

Skye ordered a Coke.

"I'll take a Coke, too, but add some rum to it." He mimed an inch with his fingers.

As the hostess walked away, Skye asked, "Is there anything you recommend?"

"I think the lobster bake is really good."

She read the description on her menu. "Oh, it has mushrooms. I don't like them."

JJ rolled his eyes. This date was turning into more work than fun.

"Wait, never mind. I read the vegetarian one. That does sound good. I'll get that." She closed her menu and laid it on the table in front of her. JJ didn't acknowledge her. He kept his head buried in his menu. The silence returned.

Their waiter arrived with their drinks. "Are you ready to order?"

In unison, they replied, "Yes."

Before Skye could say anything else, JJ told the waiter, "She'll have the lobster bake, and I'll have the crab cakes."

The waiter asked the standard questions about their salads and side dishes. He let Skye answer them for herself.

After the waiter collected the menus, Skye said, "I thought you said you wanted the lobster bake."

"No, you asked what I would recommend."

"Same thing."

"I had it the last time I was here. I like variety when I go out."

Skye responded with a nod of her head.

After another moment of silence, Skye said, "In the car, I think I worded it wrong when I said I thought you were closer to Sara's age. But the explanation in my head, sounded like you look older than you are and I didn't want to insult you. I was surprised that you're that much older than her. I'm sorry."

"It's okay. I was wondering about it though. I know a man isn't supposed to ask, but do you mind if I ask how old you are? I mean you know how old I am."

"I'm twenty-three."

He looked at her with a straight face. "Hmm," he retorted.

Neither could keep from laughing.

The laughter continued through their salads, dinner, and cheesecake for her and key lime pie for him.

Skye was raised to be independent, and she was proving she was with everything she was tackling in her life. Nevertheless, when JJ pulled out his wallet and placed his credit card on the bill, she felt she had never seen anything so manly in her life. It wasn't that he was paying for the meal. It was the action itself. Maybe it was just that JJ had done it. She was impressed with how he ate his crab cakes.

When they left the restaurant, JJ took Skye's hand in his. His touch burned throughout her body, igniting a flame in the pit of her stomach. *I thought firefighters put out fires.* She wanted to feel the burn of an intense workout. With her free hand, she reached across herself and grabbed his bicep. She pulled him into her until her face was against his arm. JJ released her hand and put his arm around her, then pulled her in close. His hand rested on her shoulder. Her hand could feel the muscles on the side of his stomach.

As they pulled up to Skye's house, she invited him in. He agreed without hesitation.

JJ held Skye's hand as they walked up to her house. He assumed it would be less obvious than his arm around her to Sara if she caught them.

The house was dark when they entered. Skye felt the wall for the light switch. They both looked at the light when it came on; a marvel of modern science. They both wore the same smile when they looked at each other.

"C'mon in." She walked into the living room, with JJ close behind. She turned on two lamps. "Can I get you something to drink?"

"Water's fine."

"Have a seat, and I'll be right back."

A thought entered Skye's head which made her nervous. *I've never had a man alone in my house before.* She had boyfriends in college who either lived in the dorms or shared an apartment, and they would be alone, but this was the first time in a place that was hers and no fear of someone walking in to the middle of anything. *I wish the anything would start already.*

She retrieved two bottles of water from her fridge then joined JJ on the sofa, both sitting on the edge. Handing him one, she said, "You did a great job in here." *Yeah, like he came in to talk shop.*

"Thanks. I'm glad you like it. I'm planning on building a fireplace similar to yours when I start the remodel on my place."

"When will that be?"

"When I get the money." JJ sat back. "I want to be able to do the whole thing at once, not a room at a time. I'd hate to finish a room, then find I have to tear out the wall to do the wiring when I do the room next to it."

Skye leaned closer. "How long do you think it will be?"

"Not long. I figure about another fifteen hundred to two-thousand, and I can start."

Skye tried every trick she knew to get JJ to kiss her. She licked her lips. She touched his arm and chest when he said something smart or amusing. She even found a way to use the word kiss in a sentence, "I love chocolate. My favorite is a Kiss." But he sat on her sofa with his arm along the back and his other on the arm or in his lap.

She was shocked when he stood up and said, "I should head home. It's getting late."

Skye jumped up. "You don't have to. I'm enjoying the conversation."

"I work tomorrow. I was supposed to work today but switched days with a guy." He looked at his watch. "I have to be up in a little over six hours."

"I understand." She tried to not look dejected as she walked him to the door. "Thank you. I had a good time."

"I had a good time, too."

JJ leaned in.

Finally.

And hugged her.

She closed the door behind him. Skye lifted her hand to her mouth and breathed out to try to smell her own breath. She smelled her underarms. She wondered as she got ready for bed what she had done to make JJ not kiss her goodnight.

CHAPTER SIXTEEN

The letters "JJ" could be seen in the doodle if anyone looked closely enough. Skye had been drawing on the pad which sat next to the register for at least an hour. She sat on the stool, head in hand, drawing circles and squares, with a few hearts that she attempted to hide whenever Gwen came near.

"So, who is he?" Gwen asked.

"Who?"

Gwen leaned on the opposite side of the counter. "The guy who has your attention today."

"No one."

"Bad date?"

"No, that's the problem. It started off bad, because I said something stupid. But once I cleared it up, it was great."

"Then why was it a bad date?"

"It didn't end well."

"Bad kisser?"

Skye shrugged. "I dunno."

Gwen stood up "What do you mean you don't know?"

Skye pulled the right side of mouth back to her ear. "He didn't kiss me."

Putting her hands on her hips, Gwen asked, "Then why didn't you kiss him?"

"What? I couldn't kiss him first." She sat up straight.

Gwen crossed her arms. "And why not?"

Skye shrugged. "Because he's the guy."

"That's your reason?"

"Sure. The guy always kisses first."

Gwen cocked her head to the side. "Well if that were true, I'd still be waiting on a first kiss."

"You know what I mean."

"No, I don't. The next time you see him, plant a big wet one on his lips."

Skye sighed. "If there is a next time. He didn't say he wanted to see me again."

"Do you have his number?"

"Yeah."

"Do you have a phone?"

"Yeah."

"Do you know how to use it?"

Skye made a 'that's a stupid question' look. "Of course."

"Then you call him and ask him out."

"I couldn't do that…could I?"

"You were brave enough to keep living after your daddy died, moved across the country by yourself and buy a house and this shop. You're more than brave enough to push some buttons on a phone."

* * *

Gwen didn't know that it was Skye's fear, not bravery, which had propelled her to this point. Dialing a phone for this call scared her. She wasn't sure if she could survive the embarrassment if he said no. She stared at her phone, set it down, and leaned back on the sofa. "How do guys get the nerve up to do this? It would kill me."

Her phone rang. "Hello."

"Hey." It was JJ.

Skye's heartrate sped up. "Hi."

"How are you?"

"I'm good. Aren't you at work?" Skye stood up and roamed around the living room.

"I am."

"And you can call me?"

"I'm in the Fire Department, not the Secret Service. We're allowed to make calls." After Skye giggled and some small talk about their day, JJ said, "I had a really good time last night."

A smile covered Skye's face, "Me, too."

"I realized after I left that I didn't ask you if you'd like to go out again."

Yes, yes. A hundred times yes! "That would be great."

"Is tomorrow too soon?"

Skye was breathless, "Tomorrow is perfect."

"Great. I'll pick you up about six?"

"Can we make it six fifteen? I close by myself tomorrow."

"Six fifteen works for me."

They hung up. Skye squealed and did what looked like running in place at high speed. "Tomorrow's gonna be a good day."

CHAPTER SEVENTEEN

Skye danced around the store, rag in hand, dusting each figurine. She sang along to every song that came on the overhead speaker. The music was a few decibels below shaking the figures off their glass shelf. It was loud enough that she didn't hear Gwen unlock the door and come in. Nor did she hear her walk across the room and right up behind her.

"The music's loud."

Skye screamed and turned, dropping the birthday cake figure, "What the hell? Don't sneak up on me like that."

Gwen laughed. "I didn't sneak up on you. You couldn't hear me. What are you so happy about? Oh, wait. Did you kiss the mystery man?"

"No, but we're going out tonight."

Gwen walked into the office to shut off the music. When she returned, she told Skye, "Make sure you plant a big wet one on him, so I don't have to watch you mope around here tomorrow."

"I promise."

* * *

It had been a good day, as Skye predicted the night before. She could tell by the cash register that it would turn out to be one the best days since she bought the shop. The only thing standing between her and an evening with JJ was a woman who roamed around the store. She was the last customer and didn't want to leave, Skye was positive of this. The woman picked up a figurine. Then put it down. She'd take two steps, then pick up another, oohing and ahing as she did. *Pick one and go already.*

The woman smiled at Skye as she set a cat statue back in its place. "I could spend hours looking at everything you have."

Lucky me. She fake-smiled at her lingering customer.

"I just love this one." The woman held up a statue of a young boy holding a stuffed bunny rabbit. "But I don't see a price on it."

"The price is on the box below it." *Buy it and leave.*

The woman was like a child finding the golden egg in an Easter egg hunt. "Oh, yes I must have this one." She grabbed the box and figurine then carried them to the register where Skye had stationed herself.

Finally.

"This one reminds me of my nephew. He's three and has a stuffed bunny like this one. But his bunny is brown, not white."

"Uh huh."

"He takes it everywhere. His father says he'll probably take it to college with him. Wouldn't that be adorable?"

"Yes, adorable. $18.73, please."

"He's not really my nephew. He's my niece's son, so he's my great-nephew. I'm sorry. How much is it?"

"$18.73."

"Do you take checks?"

Skye wasn't sure if the growl she heard in her head could be heard by the lady or not. "Yes, we do…with proper ID."

"Oh, I'll just charge it."

The woman continued to ramble on about her great-nephew as she pulled a credit card out of her wallet and handed it to Skye. Before releasing it, she said, "You look familiar. Have we met before?"

"I just moved here a few weeks ago. I don't remember meeting you."

"And you have the prettiest eyes."

She glanced at the card. The name stared back at her - Alice Vandermeer. Her body froze. Her stomach came alive. *Oh, my God.*

"Is there something wrong?"

"No, I…I misread the expiration date."

Skye finished the transaction then handed the woman a bag containing her new treasure. "Thank you."

"You're welcome. I promise I'll be back soon."

"That's great. We love repeat customers."

Skye followed the woman to the door, who stopped when she realized Skye was closing for the evening.

"Oh, I'm sorry. You're trying to go home, and I was dilly-dallying. Sometimes I just don't notice what's going on around me."

"You're fine." *Mom.*

The woman continued talking. "My family tells me all the time I should pay attention to what's going on. I promise them I will, but then I don't know what happens. I think it's because I love talking with new people and don't get to meet many in this small town. You probably get to meet new people all the time."

Skye fought a hard battle, but her cheerful expression was overtaken by excitement. Her breath escaped her nose, making a loud noise the woman could not miss.

"Oh, I'm sorry. You want to go home." The woman turned and walked away.

Skye held the words inside that were trying to escape her – *Please don't go. I think I might be your daughter.* But she let the lady go. She needed more proof that she was Rose before she revealed her secret. She wiped away a tear that had found its way down her cheek.

* * *

It was almost six before Skye got home. The drive home, she kept replaying in her head seeing the woman's name, her mother's name. A stop sign was just a pole with a sign as she drove past it, wrapped in what she should have said scenarios. She wondered why today had to be the day she came in. It ripped the excitement of seeing JJ again right out from under her.

Skye didn't rush to answer her phone. It didn't matter if it went to voicemail, until she saw JJ's name. "Hello," she sang with a smile. The memory of her mother's visit to the store was wiped away with just seeing his name.

"Hey, I was wondering if my sister is home."

"I don't know."

"Can you check?"

"Sure. Why?"

Skye walked to her front window as JJ explained, "I don't want her to see me pick you up."

She moved the curtain. "Both cars are there."

"Dammit. Would you think I was horrible if I had you meet me?"

"Yes, I would, but I'll do it anyway. I don't know how to get there, though."

"When your road ends, turn right."

Skye interrupted. "My road ends?"

"Yeah. If you go past Sara's house about six blocks, it ends at Graham." He continued, while she jotted down what he said. "It's only ten minutes or so."

"Okay. I got it. I'll see you in about half an hour?"

JJ agreed, and she hung up. Skye checked herself in the mirror. Her hair flowed over her shoulders. She went to her room and retrieved a hair tie. She pulled her hair up into a ponytail, but let her bangs hang free. She held them in front of her nose, contemplating cutting them, but decided to let them be for now.

Grabbing her purse, she headed out the door. She looked at Sara's house to see if JJ would have been caught. She didn't see her or Ty, but she knew that didn't mean they couldn't see her.

She followed JJ's directions. The drive allowed her to think about Alice Vandermeer in her store. She second guessed not telling her suspicion of who she was, even though she knew that it would have been the wrong thing to do, especially then. *Hi, Alice Vandermeer. I'm your daughter, Rose Vandermeer.*

JJ didn't tell her what they were doing, just the name of the place. She made the right into Jarrod's. Skye saw him leaning against his car. She pulled into the first vacate parking spot, two away from him.

JJ was standing next to her by the time she put the car into park. She didn't try to hide her smile. He opened her door when she unlocked it.

"Hi," they said together.

Taking Skye's hand, JJ asked if she had ever played miniature golf.

"A few times when I was little, but I haven't done it in years. My dad used to take me."

JJ pointed to a bucket of golf balls. "Pick a color." As soon as she grabbed one, JJ protested. "No, not that one."

Skye looked at it. "Why not?"

"I always use blue."

"But I like blue."

"No, I always have blue balls." The guy behind the counter laughed. Skye saw the red cover JJ's face.

"I'm sorry to hear that," Skye snickered.

JJ shook his head. "I always use the blue golf ball when I'm here," he clarified.

Skye tried not to laugh as she handed it to him. "I guess you have blue balls because I gave it to you."

"Well, actually, if you did, I wouldn't."

The same shade of red covered her face. She picked a golf ball that matched her now glowing cheeks.

After four holes, JJ had a large lead. Skye stuck out her bottom lip and pretended to pout. "No fair. You're not letting me win."

"I didn't know I was supposed to."

"Well, you at least have to give me a chance. Teach me." She held out her golf club.

"Come here. I'll show you."

Skye walked to him. JJ turned her around, by grabbing her shoulders. He placed his arms around her and wrapped his hands over hers. As he bent over, so her putter reached the ground, her bottom pressed against him. She smiled at the throaty noisy that she forced out of him.

JJ explained as he moved her arms with his. "Make sure you have a nice, even, continuous swing. Keep the head straight and hit the ball with the center of it." They watched as her ball went over the bridge and stopped inches from the hole.

When JJ took his turn, he hit his ball over the bridge. It stopped short of Skye's ball. He told her, "You're closer."

Skye got hers in on her next try. JJ took three tries to get his in.

As the game progressed, she caught up and took the lead. She hugged him whenever she'd win a hole. His smile suggested he was letting her win.

Skye won by two strokes. "Ha, I won. Now you owe me dinner."

"I don't remember making that bet."

Skye smiled. "It doesn't matter. You lost. You have to buy dinner."

JJ embraced her. They stood face-to-face. Skye's lips begged for his. He hadn't kissed her at the end of their first date, and she was now wondering if he'd do it this time.

He grinned. "Okay, but I get to pick where."

Skye didn't protest his declaration but objected to him letting go without a kiss. *Are you kidding me? What the hell?* She was sure he liked her. Well, pretty sure. Okay, she knew she affected him physically. When he held her to show her how to putt better, he had proven it.

JJ took Skye's hand. He led her to the hut where he had embarrassed himself earlier to return their putters. His previous faux pas was gone from her head. The thought of his hand wrapped around hers blocked everything else out of her brain.

He led her to the parking lot. "Do you want to just take my car or do you want to follow me?"

She knew riding with JJ meant more time with him. "We can take your car."

JJ opened the car door and held her hand as she slid in. He closed her door and went around the back of the car. He got into the car and started it. "You'll love this place."

"And if I don't?"

"Well, I hope you do, 'cause I do." He twisted in his seat to back out of the spot.

They drove a short distance, but Skye was lost. She had never been to this part of town and couldn't find her way back to her car on her own. She watched as restaurants past her window. She remembered once telling her father that close rides feel longer when you don't know where you're going. She could see his smile as he agreed with her.

Skye sat up when JJ turned into the parking lot of a strip mall. There was a fast food place and what appeared to be a fancy restaurant – neither were dressed appropriately for it. The only option she saw was the burger place, disappointing to say the least.

JJ pulled into a parking spot across the parking lot from both restaurants. Skye couldn't see any place to eat. JJ got out of the car. Skye scanned the businesses. She saw a restaurant tucked in the corner between the grocery store and the rest of the strip mall. The front wall matched the bricks of the grocery store, which sat out at least ten feet further than the other businesses. It had a large window with a blinking open sign. The front door was wooden, with a large decorative metal handle. To her, it seemed as though it would fit perfectly on a medieval castle. JJ pulled the door open.

Inside was nothing Skye expected. Hidden behind the door was an Italian restaurant, complete with red and white tablecloths and candles in the middle of the table. If the smell was an indication of how the food tasted, she knew it would be good. JJ led her past the "Please wait to be seated" sign to a table in the back.

"Do you like lasagna?"

"I love it. It's one of my favorite foods."

"Then you'll love it from here."

The waiter walked up to their table. "Didn't you see the "Please wait to be seated" sign?"

"Of course, I saw it. I had to walk around it."

Skye wished she had a menu to hide behind.

"How ya doin, JJ?" the waiter asked as he extended his hand.

JJ shook his hand as he replied. "I'm good, Tony. You?"

"I'm okay." He turned his attention to Skye. "Did you lose a bet to have to be seen with him in public?"

"No," Skye blushed.

"If you're being held against your will, blink twice."

Skye giggled as JJ introduced them. "Tony and I went to high school together. He's the owner of this dump. I only eat here to make him feel good."

"I thought you said he had the best lasagna," Skye countered.

"You're supposed to help me, not him," JJ quipped.

"Two lasagnas. What can I get you to drink?"

JJ pointed to Skye, "Red wine?" She nodded. "Two glasses of red wine and be quick about it." He snapped his fingers in the air.

"Bite me," Tony said as he walked away.

They laughed and smiled. They touched each other. Skye rubbed her hand over his bicep. Tony checked on them a few times to see what else they wanted. After two glasses of wine both switched to Coke – JJ because he was driving and Skye because JJ did. Skye didn't want the night to end and hoped JJ felt the same. They sat talking, not paying attention to the time until Tony interrupted them again.

Tony pointed to JJ, "Okay, you," switching to his thumb, "get out." He turned to Skye, "I'm sorry, but we closed twenty minutes ago."

Skye's cheeks filled with color. "I'm sorry. I didn't mean to keep you."

Tony replied, "Don't apologize. It's cool. I have to get home to my wife."

JJ's face lit up. "Oh yeah, I forgot to ask. How's she doing?"

"Tired and moody, due in two weeks."

They shook hands. "Good luck with that."

JJ wrapped his arm around Skye as he led her to the door. *Finally!* She lifted her arm to around his waist. They went out the door sideways, so they didn't have to break contact. And just like when she got in the car earlier, he opened her door and held her hand as she got it.

They held hands the entire drive back. Skye wished his car didn't have bucket seats, so she could move closer to him. The ride back felt shorter than the trip there. She didn't want the night to end.

JJ pulled up behind her car, blocking in hers and the ones on either side of hers. They walked hand-in-hand the eight short steps to her car door.

"I had fun tonight." She tried to look at him, but one of the lights illuminating the mini golf course blinded her. She moved to be able to see his face.

"Me, too."

His smile generated a voltage that traveled through her body. "Thank you for a great time."

"Can we do it again…soon?"

There was no reason for his question to embarrass her, but she could feel the warmth of reddening cheeks. "I'd like that."

He wrapped his arms around her. She put her hands on his chest. She looked like she was pushing him away, when inside she wanted to pull him closer. JJ looked around the parking lot, as though they were acting suspiciously. Then he told her, "Normally, I wouldn't do this…the garlic and all…but I can't help myself."

Her eyes closed as his mouth covered hers. Her body melted into his. Her hands followed his chest to over his collarbone, up his neck, into his black hair. One hand brushed his ear. His hand opened against her back and pulled her closer. She was thankful he was holding her. She was sure her legs would give out without him supporting her.

When he pulled away, he didn't stand up. Instead, his head hung down near her face. "I'll call you tomorrow."

Skye smiled and nodded. "Yeah."

He kissed her again before opening her car door. "Talk to you tomorrow." Then he closed the door.

She watched him walk back to his car, get in, start it, then pull forward.

CHAPTER EIGHTEEN

Skye returned to the Gable and Ell house that was the town's library. The night before she dreamt of JJ and his kiss. However, this morning, her thoughts were centered around the woman who may be her mother. She needed a little help getting started from the brown and grey-haired librarian getting started again. After she walked away, Skye started her search.

Skye found pictures of Rose. She even discovered an age-progressed picture which didn't reveal enough to prove yes or no. She found a picture of the toddler's mother, Alice. There was no denying she was the woman in her store the day before, but she couldn't find anything that told who Skye was. She found a picture of the toddler's father.

This time she paid more attention to the father's picture. He didn't look like the man she called daddy. This man was skinnier and had no facial hair. The image would get blurry as she stared at it. She'd close her eyes, open them slowly, then stare again. The more she looked at it, the more she believed the pain medication made her father hallucinate and she was not the kidnapped toddler, Rose Vandermeer.

This time, she printed out the pictures and articles. She believed having them at home, she could read them without any strangers hovering nearby. She had the perfect cover story, "I bought the Vandermeer house and I was wondering what happened." However, she knew she couldn't research for an extended time without the librarian getting suspicious. And in the privacy of her own home, without the chance of anyone recognizing her.

CHAPTER NINETEEN

JJ smiled when he saw Skye. Her tight green dress accented her in just the right places. He looked down at his jeans and polo shirt. Skye was dressed for a night on the town. JJ was dressed for a pizza. "You look amazing."

The corners of Skye's mouth turned upward.

"I am really underdressed."

"No, you look nice." Skye avoided eye contact with JJ. She used her left hand to play with the fingers on her right hand. "I must have misunderstood you. I thought you said we were going to someplace nice."

JJ's smile transformed into a chuckle. "No, I said, 'A nice place.'"

She shrugged. "That's what I said."

"I forgot you're still new here. A Nice Place is a restaurant."

"I figured that. You said we were going to eat."

JJ shook his head. "No, that's the name of the restaurant."

Skye felt the familiar hue of her cheeks change shades of red, their natural state whenever she was around JJ. "I didn't know. I'll go change." She turned around. Before she could take a step, JJ reached for her.

"Don't change. You look so beautiful. We'll stop by my place, and I'll change."

Skye protested, but JJ stood his ground until she relented. She grabbed her clutch off the telephone table next to the front door. He opened the screen door, both arms now fully extended. One held the doorknob, the other held the screen door for them. JJ shifted to allow Skye to lock her front door. The heels she was wearing fooled her into believing she was eye level with him, although looking straight ahead, her eyes rested on his perfect chin.

Skye glanced toward Sara's house as they walked to the car. She and JJ had agreed they would say it was their first date, no matter how many times they had been out together if Sara caught them. JJ chuckled as he attempted to count the number of blind dates he had endured thanks to his sister.

They drove to JJ's place. Skye couldn't imagine how his place would look, even though she had tried countless times. He spoke of his house, but she envisioned an apartment, or renting one floor of a house. She saw the house that needed to be painted and smiled to herself. It was what she pictured when she thought about him renting one floor.

"I'll be five minutes. Do you want to come in?"

Skye nodded.

JJ hopped out of his car and ran around to the other side in time to offer his hand to help Skye out of the car. She took it with a smile. He held it until he needed that hand to retrieve his keys from his pocket to unlock his front door.

Skye looked around as she entered. She expected it to be a mess, but it was well-kept.

"It's not much, but it keeps me warm and dry."

"It's nice."

"Can I get you something to drink?"

Skye shook her head.

"I'll be down in five minutes. The kitchen is through there if you change your mind." He jogged up the steps before she could respond.

Skye walked around his living room, checking whatever he had out. She picked up a picture that she assumed was JJ as a teenager and his father. The two looked similar, so the other man in the picture had to be a relative. After she circled the room, she sat in a chair that faced his front door. She heard him come down the steps.

When he appeared at the bottom, she froze. He donned a dark blue suit, light blue shirt, and a paisley tie. She had no words because her brain had failed her.

"Do I look that bad?" he asked as he walked to her.

"No, you look fantastic.

JJ smiled. "Thanks. Ready? Let's go." He grabbed Skye's hand and led her out the door and to the car.

As JJ backed out of his driveway, Skye asked, "So where are we going?"

"I was thinking about the steakhouse up the road. Sound good?"

"That sounds fantastic. I haven't had a good steak in a while."

"Then you'll love this place."

They held hands on the drive to the restaurant and as they walked in. It was a weeknight, so they were seated after a short wait. Skye touched his chest when she spoke.

The hostess seated them at a table near the decorative waterfall then took their drink orders.

Skye thought for a moment. "Vodka and cranberry juice, please."

"Bourbon, neat."

This is a real man. Not like the boys I dated in college who ordered, "What do you have on tap?" Bourbon. That's a man's drink.

Skye opened her menu, then laughed.

"What?"

"Is this their real menu?"

"Of course, it is. Why?"

"The prices. I can't let you pay this much."

"Don't worry about the prices. It's okay, or I wouldn't have brought you here."

Skye opened her mouth, but JJ stopped her before she could speak. She went back to studying her menu. They both ordered the surf and turf – Skye's with shrimp, JJ's with the lobster. Graduating college, her father's death, purchasing a house and buying a business hadn't made her feel as much a woman as this one meal. Her other dates had all been playing grown-up when compared to this one. There was serious adult conversation with smiles and laughs. These were the mature laughs, where Skye would cover her mouth, and JJ's eyes lit up, and his smile broadened.

Over dessert – chocolate torte for her and tiramisu for him – Skye told JJ the story of her father's death. When she'd get tears in her eyes, he'd tell her, "You don't have to tell me anymore." But she continued until she reached the part of buying Bric-A-Brac. She finished with, "And you know the rest."

"Want to know my favorite part of that story?"

Skye thought it was odd that he'd have a favorite part of her father dying. "Okay?"

"The part where I knocked on your front door and saw you for the first time. You took my breath away."

"I liked what I saw, too."

JJ leaned toward Skye and kissed her.

When they were driving home, JJ asked, "Would you like to go back to my place for a bit? We won't have to worry about Sara there."

Warmth spread throughout Skye. "That sounds good."

* * *

Inside JJ's house, he laid his jacket over the chair Skye had sat in earlier and loosened his necktie. Skye studied the CDs next to his sound system. She liked most of them.

"Would you like a drink?"

"No, thank you."

"How about the grand tour?"

"You've seen my whole house. It's only fair I see yours."

JJ went from room to room explaining how he wants to remodel each one. "I'm going to make the living room and dining room more one room. I'm going to take out the wall and replace it with four feet long, floor-to-ceiling shelves. Or something similar."

Skye watched as his eyes danced with each description. Her body moved in time to the same song. She could listen to him sing this tune all night.

When they got to his bedroom, Skye entered first and walked to the middle. JJ stayed in the doorway. He told her the only plan he had for this room was to make an entrance to the bathroom, or build a master bath, if he had the money.

"This is nice. I like 'em big."

JJ walked to her. "That's good for both of us."

Skye shook her head as she contorted her face.

"Never mind." JJ kissed her. Both pulled the other closer as his tongue found hers. Her fingers ran through his hair. His hand on the small of her back and held her against him. She could feel his excitement in her stomach.

He moved his hands to her hips and pulled at it to lift her dress.

Skye moved away. "Does that offer for a something to drink still stand?"

JJ exhaled through his nose. "Yes, it does."

"I could go for a drink now."

He nodded in agreement in a way that included his shoulders, too. "Sure." He stepped to the side to allow Skye to go first. She closed her eyes as she walked, willing her body to stop responding to his. The deep breath she took in was released as though she was blowing bubbles. She walked downstairs. It was not a hurried pace to escape the situation, but her normal gait, because she knew this was not the right time.

In the living room, JJ asked, "What would you like to drink?"

"Anything is fine."

JJ disappeared into the kitchen while Skye once again inspected his living room. She picked up a figurine she recognized and let out a "ha." She was still holding it when he returned.

"I recognize this." She held a statue of a firefighter holding a child.

"You do?" He handed her a glass of white wine.

"I sell it at my store."

"I guess that's where my mom got it then. She gave it to me when I graduated from the academy."

He gestured to the sofa, "Wanna sit down?"

Skye returned the figure to where she got before joining JJ on the couch. He moved closer to her. She paid attention to the darkened room. She hadn't seen him turn out a light on the way to sit down. She didn't mind, she just sipped her wine.

As they spoke, JJ removed his tie and tossed it onto the coffee table. He put his arm around Skye who smiled at him. He propped his feet on the table, and she snuggled closer to him. The conversation continued.

Skye shared with JJ a story of when she and her father were in a minor car accident. He kissed her on top of her head and said, "I'm glad you weren't hurt and are here with me now."

She looked up at him and said, "I'm glad I'm here, too."

Skye arched her back to accept the kiss JJ offered. His hand moved to the nape of her neck. She placed her hand on his chest. She could feel the muscles she saw under her deck. His tongue explored her mouth. She undid two buttons on his shirt and put her hands inside. JJ's hand moved to her thigh and slid it under her dress.

JJ whispered, "Do you want to go upstairs?"

Skye didn't reply with words, only a dip of her head.

He kissed her then they stood up. JJ led her by the hand to the bottom of the steps. Not letting go he offered to let her go first. They moved up the steps without rushing and without making a noise on the darkened stairs. Skye stopped at the top and waited for JJ. He reached the last step, tightened the muscles in his arm to prevent her from walking more. His free hand grasped the back of her head as his mouth found hers. He released her hand and mouth. His arm slid around her waist and he steered her toward his bedroom.

JJ flipped a light switch which turned on a small light on his nightstand. Skye looked at it and giggled.

"What?"

She continued to giggle as she spoke. "Aren't you a little old for a night light?"

JJ chuckled. "I use it when I'm watching TV in here." His mouth overtook hers before she could reply. He wrapped his arms around her. He unzipped her dress and she finished unbuttoning his shirt. JJ moved her dress off her shoulders, and she let it fall to the floor. She kissed his chest as she pushed his shirt off him. Skye sat on his bed. As she undid the straps on her heels, he unhooked his belt, then untied his shoes and removed them. He pulled the blankets back and allowed her to slide under them. She watched his hands as he peeled off his pants. He slid in beside her.

JJ moved his arm to under Skye's head, and his other hand brushed her hair out of her face. She smiled: at him, at the moment, at how she could feel how much he wanted her with her thigh. It was then that she understood his comment when they were in the room earlier. His tongue moved over her neck. Skye's body tingled. Her hands ran through his soft hair and down his back. He found the clasp of her bra which lay between her breasts, undoing it, his mouth covered one while his hand massaged the other. She let out a whimper and pulled his head closer to her chest.

As he continued to explore her body, she removed her bra and dropped it beside his bed. Her hands explored any part of his body they could reach, while her body answered his touch and kisses with sounds of contentment. JJ kissed her stomach and removed her panties.

JJ adjusted so Skye could remove his underwear. It was barely audible, but she heard him say, "Yes."

Skye did not know what to do when he broke all contact between them and rolled away. She looked down at her half-exposed body. She looked at the darkened area to her right, which was JJ's back. She heard him open and close the nightstand drawer. He rolled back to face her, ending by leaning on his elbow.

He held up a condom and said, "Gotta be safe."

She watched him push back the covers and opened the package. Skye was thankful for the small lamp. She stared at him, happy for getting to see what had lived in her thoughts for the past six weeks. Then he moved on top of her. His grey eyes made contact with hers and she saw a look that sent an electricity down her body while he pushed toward her. They both released a moan of satisfaction.

JJ maintained eye contact as he lifted up to his hands. Skye's hands roamed over his chest, stomach, and arms. She lifted onto her elbows and licked his chest. He shifted to his elbows while her tongue made circles around his nipple, quickening his pace. He moved so he could intercept her mouth with his. He moved his arms, so there was nothing between their bodies. Her tongue danced in and out of his mouth. He made a noise that echoed in his throat. He pushed her tongue back into her mouth with his.

He made the noise three more times as he breathed out fast and hard. Her heart pounded in a way she had never felt before. It reverberated between her ears. It throbbed in her stomach and reverberated down to her thighs. Skye echoed his actions.

JJ lips brushed Skye's and then he rolled onto the bed. She watched as he closed his eyes, breathed out through lips, which were almost closed, opened his eyes, then looked at her and smiled.

"I'll be right back." He gave her another kiss before getting out of bed. When he returned, Skye's eyes were closed. He spoke, but she didn't reply. He watched her chest rise and fall in a slow rhythm. As much as he wanted to wake her, he let her sleep. JJ moved slowly into bed and turned off the light. He held Skye and allowed the cadence of her breathing to move him to sleep.

CHAPTER TWENTY

Skye opened her eyes. JJ placed his hand on her cheek. His thumb stayed next to her nose while the rest of his hand moved to her jawbone. Then he stroked her cheek with his thumb.

"Good morning."

She smiled. "Good morning."

"How'd you sleep?"

"Good. You?"

"Good. I put a pair of my sweatpants and a tee shirt in the bathroom for you. There's a towel, too, if you want to shower. I don't have a spare toothbrush, but there is toothpaste in the cabinet."

"I'll just use yours."

He tilted his head, "I'd prefer you didn't."

She laughed.

"Oh…I thought about making pancakes and bacon for breakfast. How's that sound?"

"Sounds good."

JJ withdrew his hand while leaning in to kiss Skye. They smiled. He turned and walked out of the bedroom. Skye watched him leave.

She arched her back as she stretched and yawned. Looking around the room, there was no woman's touch to it. She didn't get much of a look at it the previous night. The nightstand had the small lamp, a TV remote, a clock and his watch. *I guess he wants to know what time it is.* On the dresser sat a hairbrush, deodorant, a can of body spray, a small television, and a pile of folded clothes. She suspected they were his work clothes since they were all blue. Next to his closet was a chest of drawers. There was a picture of his parents. Sara had the same one. A picture of Sara and him at her wedding and one of Sara, Ty, and Abby on the day she was born. Next to it was a Mason jar more than half-full of change.

Skye was not aware of her nakedness until she threw back the blanket. Dressed only in goose bumps and the remnants of last night's make-up, she crossed her arms in front of her chest as she hurried into the bathroom. She closed the door behind her.

The grey sweatpants he left for her bunched at her ankles and half-way up her calf. She didn't feel like going into the bedroom to get her bra, so she went without…even though the white tee shirt did little to conceal her nipples. Skye preferred to wear socks, but didn't wear any the previous night, and she didn't think she should go through his drawers to find a pair.

"Hi." Skye smiled as she entered the kitchen. "Breakfast smells great."

"Thank you. Coffee?"

"Yes, please."

JJ poured the hot black liquid into a cup which was sitting next to the coffee maker. He set it down on the island in front of an empty chair. "Sugar. Cream." He pushed each item closer to her. "Milk's in the fridge if you'd prefer that."

"These are fine. Spoon?"

"Sorry." He retrieved one from the silverware drawer and handed it to her, then turned his attention back to the pancakes.

When JJ turned back around, he had two plates, each with three pancakes and three slices of bacon. He set Skye's plate in front of her as he leaned over and kissed her. They put butter on their pancakes, then smothered them in syrup.

"Should I thank you for last night or just tell you how great it was?"

Skye put the empty fork into her mouth. She slid it out slowly. "Both."

"Don't do that."

Skye put the empty fork back into her mouth. She slid it out slower. "Don't do what?" She bit her lip.

He made a rasping sound as his eyes darted left and right. "Don't start a game you're not willing to play."

She stabbed a piece of JJ's pancake, licked the syrup, which was dripping off it, then put it into her mouth. "Mm"

JJ looked at the ceiling. He let out a breath. It had an "oh" sound. He looked back at Skye. Playful seduction danced in her eyes. She licked her lips. "What's the name of this game?"

"Twister."

"Twister, huh? Like right hand blue, left leg green? I don't have it, so how can we play?"

"Sex is nature's version of Twister. Left leg behind left ear. Right leg on his left thigh."

"If that's true, you won last night. Wanna play again?" He smirked.

Skye stood up as she grabbed JJ's hand. Her tongue touched his top lip as she kissed him. JJ wrapped his arm around her waist and pulled her closer. She stood between his thighs, his feet propped on the bottom rung of the bar stool. She could taste the syrup he had on his pancakes as his tongue pushed its way past hers. His hands held her waist, and her hands felt his chest. JJ picked her up, not in the over-the-threshold style, but lifted her straight up so he could carry and kiss her at the same time. Her legs wrapped around his waist.

In the living room, he set her down. JJ pulled his undershirt over his head and dropped it on the floor. He reached under the shirt she was wearing as he kissed her.

They both stared at each other when someone knocked on his front door.

"Go upstairs. I'll be there in a minute."

Skye went as far as the landing and watched him look through the peephole, sigh, and open the door not much wider than his face. She listened to his conversation.

"Hey. What's up?"

She heard Sara's voice. "Abby wanted to say goodbye before leaving for the cabin."

"Bye Princess. You have fun."

"JJ. Let us in."

"No"

"Come on. Open the door." Skye saw the door move from Sara pushing on it.

"Not now, Sare."

"Why not?"

"It's Saturday and look at the way I'm dressed."

"Oh…and she's still here?"

"Upstairs."

"Abby, tell Uncle JJ goodbye, and you'll see him two weeks."

Instead, Abby said, "Hug."

JJ opened the door wider. Skye couldn't see what he did, but assumed he hugged her.

Skye hurried up the steps when he said goodbye. She took off the sweats and shirt as fast as she could. JJ came into the room as she climbed under the covers. Seeing she wasn't dressed, he pulled off the pajama pants he was wearing and followed her under the covers.

Skye climbed on top of him before he could react. JJ was flat on his back. "Hello."

She replied, "Hi." She kissed him. His hands glided over her calves and up her thighs. She could still smell his shaving cream when she moved to kiss him below his ear onto his neck. She moved down his chest. Her tongue made a circle around his nipple, and he pulled her waist to get her closer to him. Skye reached down between her legs and grabbed him. She moved to him. JJ arched his back, moving away from her.

"No Baby. We can't take chances." Without looking, he opened the nightstand and pulled out a condom while Skye sat on his hips. He put it between his teeth, then moved Skye down to his thighs. She watched him rip open the package, then made it safe to make love to him again. He smiled and said, "Now," and moved her back to his hips.

JJ held Skye's hips as her movement excited him more. When she pressed her chest against his, he ran his hands up and down her back. She sat up, and he fondled her breasts. She could feel he was loving every inch of what she was doing to him. Skye ran her hands over his chest. He closed his eyes, looked up, and made an "mm" sound.

Skye laid back down on his chest. She was making the same "mm" sound in JJ's ear. He could no longer contain himself. He wrapped his arms around her and thrust his body as close to hers as possible, making the same throaty noise and short breaths as last night.

They spent the day in bed, talking and laughing. When anything important popped up, Skye and JJ handled it – it had to be handled two more times.

When JJ saw it was already sunset, he asked Skye about dinner. They decided to go to her house, so she could get dressed, then go out somewhere.

The pair held hands as they drove to Skye's house. Her dress from the previous night was in a plastic bag while she wore the sweatpants and tee shirt from earlier that day. Knowing Sara, Tyler, and Abby were on vacation they didn't have to worry about them being caught and explaining her outfit. They walked hand-in-hand into Skye's house.

"I'll just be a minute. Grab a drink if you want."

"Or I could go upstairs with you."

Skye kissed him. "If you go with me, we won't leave. Then we'll starve to death.

"But what a way to die."

Skye ran up to a bedroom, pulled on a pair of jeans, grabbed the first shirt in her closet and stepped into a pair of sandals. She ran her hairbrush through her hair and ran back downstairs.

"That was quick."

"I'm hungry." *And I love seeing your smile.*

JJ pulled Skye close when they were walking down her sidewalk to his car. He opened her door and closed it. Skye unlocked his door as he ran around to his side. JJ started the car, then held her hand as he drove to the restaurant.

They pulled up to a building that could easily be identified as a restaurant by its large plate glass windows. There were roses painted on them with the words Rose's Café. Skye was surprised at the homey feel it had. She expected harsh lighting with fast food seating. Instead, the windows had a tint that wasn't easy to see outside but was obvious on the inside. There were tables, with tablecloths, and real wooden chairs. JJ steered her to a table against a wall.

A waitress appeared with menus almost at the same time.

"Hey JJ," she said as she handed him his menu.

He looked at her as he took his. "Hey." It sounded as though it was two syllables long.

"How've you been? You haven't been over the house is a while."

"I've been good…busy. I didn't know you were working here."

The waitress looked at Skye. "I just started a few weeks ago."

"Dawn, this is Skye." He lifted his hand far enough off the table to point in her direction. "Skye, this is Dawn. She's the little sister of a friend of mine."

Skye saw Dawn roll her eyes. "Hi."

Dawn smiled and nodded. "Do you two know what you want, or do you just want to order your drinks?"

They both ordered their drinks, so they could look over the menus.

Skye flipped her menu over. She saw the same logo as on the front window, but it was the bottom right corner that took away her breath - the same picture of the toddler that was on the sign in her front yard stared back at her. She looked at JJ and said, "This is the picture from my yard."

"Yeah, the lady who owns here used to own your house. She's the girl's mother."

Skye's body trembled. *This is my mother's restaurant.*

"What looks good?"

Skye couldn't speak. She shook her head and stared at the menu. The words blurred.

Dawn returned with their drinks. She asked if they were ready to order. Skye ordered the first thing she saw, the turkey dinner, and JJ asked for the steak dinner. Because Skye had never had fried pickles, JJ got an order as an appetizer.

JJ placed both hands on the table, and Skye held them. "I've had a great day with you."

His words forced her out of her stupor. "Only because we spent it in bed."

"You really think I'm that shallow?"

She let go of one of his hands and flicked her wrist. "I'm just joking with you. I had a great day, too."

They chatted until Dawn brought the pickles. She set them in front of JJ. "Do you need anything else?"

He looked at Skye, who shook her head. "Nope, we're good."

Dawn dropped her head, then walked away.

As JJ moved the basket to the middle of the table, Skye said, "She has a crush on you."

He looked to his left and right, as though she was speaking to someone else. "Who? Dawn? Nah. I've known her since she was in kindergarten. She's like a kid sister to me."

Skye took a bite of a pickle. "Mm, not bad. She looks at you like more than a big brother."

"I told you they were good. Here, try the dip. Why do you say that?"

Skye reached for the dip with the pickle she had already bitten. JJ pulled it back. "No double dipping."

"She lit up when she saw you, and I haven't dipped this one yet." She popped it into her mouth.

JJ looked around the restaurant and found Dawn peeking at him over the decorative wall between the seating area and the waitress' area. He looked back at Skye. "Damn, I've never noticed it before." Skye was eating the pickles while JJ was talking. "Hey, save some for me." He pulled the basket back to him.

Skye studied half of JJ's face. He was looking at Dawn, who would glance at him.

"Did you bring me here to get a reaction?"

"What do you mean?"

"From Dawn." *Or do you know my secret and wanted to see how I'd react here.*

"No, really. I had no clue she liked me."

They stopped speaking when they saw Dawn coming with their food. There wasn't much talking while they ate. JJ was quiet because he was shoveling his food into his mouth. Skye wasn't saying anything because she was afraid of what words might escape her.

A lady walked up to their table. "Hi, how's everything this evening?"

"Fantastic as always," JJ replied with a smile.

The lady smiled and turned her attention to Skye, who replied, "It's good."

"I'm happy to hear it. If there's anything I can do, please let me know. My name is Alice, and I'm the owner. She looked at Skye and ducked her chin into her chest to see her better. "You look familiar. Have you been in before?"

Oh my God! She recognizes me. Her voice quivered, "No." She stared at the woman's face trying to find something, anything that resembled her face, anything she missed when she visited her store.

"I know I've seen you."

A lead ball pressed down in her stomach. Skye closed her eyes slowly. *Don't vomit on her.* "I don't know from where," she lied. *Please stop. I'm not ready for a reunion.* She placed her fork on her plate and used her left hand to play with the fingers on her right hand.

The woman lifted one finger and pointed at Skye. "I know where I know you from."

Skye's eyes widened. She swallowed hard to hold down the vomit. Her heart pounded. She could hear the blood rush past her ears. She fought to keep her expression friendly instead of the horror she was experiencing.

"You work at the figurine store."

Skye deflated. *Thank God.* "Yes, I own it."

"I love that place."

"Thank you."

The lady promised to come in again before excusing herself to visit with other customers.

Skye told JJ, "Excuse me," as she stood up. She went into the bathroom, locked the door behind her, then went into the stall. "Oh my God! Oh my God! Oh my God!" She leaned over the toilet, one hand on the wall, the other on the metal divider. She stood up and shook her hands while still repeating, "Oh my God!" Skye exited the stall and walked to the sink. She braced herself on it. She looked at the eyes that reflected back at her. "Relax. She doesn't know who you are. Pull yourself together before JJ gets suspicious. Unless he already is. He could have brought you here on purpose. No. You can't think that way. He doesn't know. There's no way he could know." She took a deep breath. Skye stood up straight, then returned to JJ who was finished eating.

"You were gone awhile. You okay?"

"Yes. My phone rang while I was in there. I didn't want to be rude and carry on a conversation in front of you." She touched her pocket to make sure her phone was there, and it couldn't have rung while she was in the bathroom.

"Thanks."

Dawn brought JJ a piece of chocolate cake. "Would you like some dessert?"

Skye's head bounced back and forth. "No thank you."

She finished eating while JJ dug into his chocolate cake. Instead of coffee, they opted for another soft drink. Skye asked JJ more about his remodeling plans while they finished their drinks.

Skye stood behind JJ when he paid. She liked the view when he pulled out his wallet and replaced it. It also kept her from having to look at the owner. She didn't have to hide her smile. He couldn't see what she was doing. She didn't even flinch when she saw Dawn's eyes darting between her and JJ's derriere.

JJ took Skye's hand as they walked to the door. He pushed it open with his free arm. Once they were outside, he pulled her close to him and wrapped his arm around her shoulder. She looked up him and smiled, then she wrapped her arm around his waist.

Like every time before, he opened her car door, offered his hand to help her in, and closed her door. However, this time, instead of watching him walk around to his side, she stared at the painted window. She saw the woman who might be her mother at the cash register helping another customer. Skye wanted to go tell her who she thought she was. She wanted to slide down in the seat so the woman couldn't see her. She wanted more time with her father to find out if he was telling the truth or just babbling in his medicated state.

JJ took a different route back to her house, through an area of town she hadn't yet explored. This trip through the neighborhood couldn't be counted as seeing. Her mind was still back at Rose's Café. When he turned into a parking lot, she perked up and took in where they were.

"This is where I work."

"Nice bricks and windows."

He looked at her and smirked. "This is the outside of where I work."

Skye giggled. "Still nice bricks and windows."

JJ breathed out through his nose as he shook his head. He put the car into gear and pulled back out onto the street.

"What I don't get to go in?"

"If I take you in, they'll assume I just have you there to impress you so you'll fuck me."

Skye's face reddened.

"I'm sorry. That's what they'd say, and I forget to filter myself."

He told her more about his job on the ride back to her house. "I joined when I was nineteen. I did a year of college before joining. No one was surprised when I did. I used to hang out at the station where my father worked when I was growing up."

His story mesmerized her. There was nothing special about it, but it was JJ's story, and she wanted to know it. His words washed away the fear and trauma of earlier.

JJ held her close when he walked her to her door. He kissed her at the front door after she unlocked it.

"Aren't you coming in?"

"If I do, I may not leave."

Skye played with the material on his shirt next to the buttons. "Would that be a bad thing?"

"Tonight it would be." His words disappointed her. "I work tomorrow."

She protested.

"Sorry, but fires don't take weekends off.'

She hugged him, her ear pressed against his chest. He held her against him. "Come over when you get off work?"

"I get off at eight Monday morning. And I've got a painting job to do that day."

"I don't want to wait to see you again." Fear engulfed her. *What if he doesn't feel the same way?*

JJ tightened his hold and kissed her head. "I wish I could stay. I don't want to wait until Tuesday to see you either."

She didn't think, she blurted out, "Come over Monday. I'll make dinner."

He looked at her, their faces almost touching. "I don't know how late I'll be. I promised I'd finish the project on Monday no matter how long it took."

"I don't care. Come over when you're done."

He kissed her lips. "Okay."

One more kiss then he walked to his car. JJ stopped at the gate and turned to her house. "Go inside," he ordered.

She waved and went in, locking the door behind her. Her heart raced at any memory of the past thirty hours, although part of it was a race she wished she could be scratched from. Skye decided to reread the articles she had copied at the library and study the pictures more. Seeing pictures of Alice Vandermeer wouldn't give her any new information. However, it gave her more incentive to find out if she was indeed her mother.

She went to bed that night with a smile and hope.

CHAPTER TWENTY-ONE

A noise Skye couldn't identify woke her. But as her head cleared, she remembered she had changed her ringtone. She answered it without focusing on the name. There was no denying the call had woken her. "Hello."

"Good morning."

Her lips curled upward in response to the sound of JJ's voice. "Good morning."

"I'm sorry I woke you, but I wanted to talk to you before I went to work."

Last night's panic overtook her body. *He knows the truth and going to tell me he's going to the police. I knew last night was a test.* Her voice quivered, "Is everything okay?"

"Everything's good. I just wanted to hear your voice."

"What time is it?"

"Six forty-two."

"Six forty? Ugh."

"Six forty-two."

"Close enough." Skye adjusted her pillow to support her back then sat up. "What time do you have to leave for work?"

"Seven thirty. But I still need to shower. What do you have planned for today?"

"Sleeping until noon."

"I'm sorry. Want me to let you go back to sleep?"

She pulled up her knees and leaned into them. "No."

"Good."

"Tell me something. What do you normally wear to bed?"

"I'm wearing pajama bottoms and an undershirt. What are you wearing?"

"Same thing, except I have pajama shorts."

"Mm, I'd like to see that."

"One day."

This led them to talking about the time in bed the day before. Skye reclined on her pillow again. JJ stopped the conversation when he said, "I hate to say it, but it's after seven. I have to jump in the shower before I'm late."

"Are you still coming over tomorrow?"

"Definitely." He paused. "There's another reason I called."

Oh no. Here it comes.

"I hope you don't think I'm crazy, or maybe I am crazy..." JJ breathed loud enough for her to hear. "I love you, Skye."

Her whole face lit up as she smiled. "Then I'm crazy, too, cause I love you, too, JJ."

"I really have to go now, though."

"Okay. Have a good day and be safe."

"I will."

Skye listened to JJ hit the end button. She hugged her cell phone. She laid down again. She replayed JJ telling her he loved her over and over in her head. It could have been half an hour. It could have been two hours she was awake thinking about him, but when she opened her eyes again it was a little before noon. She thought for a moment that she had dreamt what he said. When she checked her phone, she saw the last call received was from JJ and lasted twenty-seven minutes. It was real. JJ was in love with her.

* * *

After lunch and trading her pajama shorts for a pair of jeans, she spread the information she had found so far about Rose's kidnapping on the coffee table. It wasn't much: four articles about the kidnapping, a picture of Rose's father, and a note to remind herself that her father wasn't in the high school yearbook under either name.

JJ loves me. "No, I have to concentrate on this."

Skye opened the picture of her father she had on her phone. She sat it next to the picture of Rose's father. She studied it. She couldn't tell if the hair color was right or not from the black and white picture in the newspaper. The eyes seemed similar. But a dot matrix picture next to an eight megapixel wasn't a good comparison.

Skye got up and walked across the kitchen, then retrieved a pencil from a drawer. She grabbed a bottle of water since she was next to the fridge. *JJ loves me.* She smiled as she recalled his early morning call.

Returning to the table, she sat down, then moved the picture of Rose's father to in front of her. She stared at his eyes, looking for a resemblance to her father's or hers. She colored in the shape of her father's beard and moustache. Her drawing on the picture made it more difficult to tell if they were the same person; all the erasing she had done to get the beard right ruined the picture.

I wonder how JJ would look with a beard. "Stop it. You have to figure this out."

She tried rereading the articles again, but her mind would find a word in the article and associate it with JJ. Then she'd have to reread what she had already reread. Skye gave up on trying to figure out the mystery of who she and her father were. She preferred the happy thoughts of JJ loving her.

CHAPTER TWENTY-TWO

Skye was in the middle of mashing potatoes when JJ knocked. She wiped her hands on the towel that hung from a handle on the oven door then hurried to answer the door. She opened the door and looked him over. She loved what she saw.

"Come in."

"I brought this." JJ kissed her. "You didn't say what you were making, so I hope it goes with it." He showed her a bottle of red wine.

"It doesn't. I have to get back into the kitchen." She returned to the kitchen with JJ right behind.

"It smells fantastic. What's on the menu?"

Skye opened the oven. "Stuffed baked pork chops," she looked at him, "apple stuffing," she looked back at the pork chops, "mashed potatoes with gravy and green bean almandine." She closed the oven.

"Sounds as good as it smells."

"Do you want something to drink?"

Still holding the bottle of wine, JJ lifted it and said, "Wine?"

"Sure."

JJ opened the wine to let it breathe. He grabbed two glasses out of her cabinet since he already knew where she kept them. He found them when he was looking for one to get a drink of water while doing the work there. He poured two glasses and gave her one.

Skye stirred the gravy and JJ leaned with his back against the counter. They shared how their day went. When

JJ asked what she had done the day before, she replied, "Nothing, just sat around the house. How was work?"

"It was quiet. There was an accident, but we weren't needed. I hate when we get called for stupid stuff. No fire. No one was injured. One car had some paint scraped off."

"I'm sorry." She walked to JJ and wrapped her arms around him. He grabbed onto her waist and kissed her. "I need to get the plates from behind you."

"Damn. I thought you did that because you liked me."

"I do. Otherwise, I would have just asked you to move."

"Do it again and then I'll move."

They kissed.

"There's white wine in the fridge. Would you get it out for us?" She plated their food while JJ got the wine. "I have tea, soda, and water in there too, if you'd prefer something else."

He told her he preferred the wine. "I'm going to let you get me drunk and take advantage of me tonight."

With a plate in both hands, she walked to him. "Do I have to get you drunk to take advantage of you?"

"Not in the least. It just makes it more fun." JJ held the glasses of wine in each hand. They held each other as best they could with food and drink in hand and kissed, their tongues softly touching the other.

They ate dinner in her dining room, with candles to enhance the mood. "This is the first time I've eaten in here. I normally eat in the kitchen or in the living room."

"So, you saved your virginity for me?"

"You wish."

"Yes, I do." He lifted his wine glass as though making a toast.

Skye rolled her eyes and shook her head.

I wonder if Daddy told the truth about where he went to college. If so, then maybe I can get information about him from there. Stop thinking about this. Pay attention to JJ.

"Is Wednesday good for you?"

Shit. What did he ask? "Sure, of course. I get off at five, like normal."

"Wednesday at six then it is."

Crap.

The candles grew smaller as Skye and JJ talked. They moved into the living room to be more comfortable, leaving the dishes on the table.

Skye snuggled under JJ's arm, after she slipped off her shoes. She did a dissertation on one of her suppliers whose had given a hard time the past few times they spoke. "I think he doesn't like dealing with me because I'm a girl."

"He doesn't know what he's missing. I happen to love the fact that you're a girl."

Skye's laugh was interrupted by JJ's kiss. He slid his free hand behind her neck to pull her closer. Her hand found his chest. She unfastened a button, so she could slip her hand inside. She stood up and reached for his hands and pulled to get him to stand up.

"What?" His smile told her he knew what she wanted.

"Let's go upstairs."

"Do you have protection?"

"No."

JJ sighed. "As much as I'd love to, I can't."

Skye sat back down. "Are you serious?"

He nodded.

"I promise it's okay now."

"I can't. One pregnancy before I'm ready for kids is enough for me."

Skye's face looked like she smelled a skunk. "Huh?"

JJ explained, "Three years ago I was serious with someone. We had been together for about a year, talking about getting married. She told me it was okay, and I slept with her. Six weeks later she told me she was pregnant. I should have caught on when she told me I now had a reason to marry her."

"She trapped you?"

"That was her plan. I bought her a ring, and we decided to get married on our one-year anniversary. I was working two days before, when we got a call for a sick case. It was her. She was having a miscarriage."

"Oh JJ. I'm so sorry."

"Thanks. I was upset when it happened, but the more I thought about it, the angrier I got. She wanted to be married and was going to go to any length to make sure she was. If she would lie to me about that, who knows what else she would lie about. So, I broke it off, but never do anything without a condom now."

"That sucks…what she did, not the condom thing. Do you ever see her anymore?"

"She moved away. She came to my place, crying, hoping I'd take her back, but I wanted nothing to do with her after that. So, she left."

"I'm sorry that happened to you." Skye hugged him and held him. She felt he needed her and didn't let go until he moved away. He kissed her.

They continued where they'd left off; his hand behind her neck, her hand in his shirt. She unbuttoned his shirt and kissed his chest. He pressed his body into the sofa and closed his eyes. He put his hand under her chin and raised her face to his. He kissed her, his tongue probing deep into her mouth. He pulled her shirt off, then laid her on the sofa. His mouth moved from hers, to her neck, down to her breast. He liked that Skye's bras hooked in the front.

JJ's hands seemed to be on automatic pilot, as if there was no connection between his brain and what he was doing. He removed her pants and underwear as he continued to kiss her body. Her fingers ran through his hair, pulling him closer when he hit a spot that excited her more. She was on the edge of ecstasy when he stopped and stood up. Her body pleaded for him to not stop then. She watched him walk away.

"Bathroom," he said without looking back.

Skye stayed on the sofa until she heard him reach the top step. She didn't wait for any reason other than wanting to hear him move around her house. She got up and put on her underwear and shirt, then went into the kitchen for something to drink. JJ joined her in there. He walked to the fridge and got a bottled water.

"Make yourself at home, why not?"

"Really?"

"I'm kidding." She walked to him and put one arm around him and laid her head on his chest.

He kissed the top of her head. "I love you."

"I was wondering if you were going to say it. I thought you reconsidered yesterday morning's call."

JJ snickered. "Nope and I have no excuse for not saying it earlier." He pulled her in closer. "Well?"

She looked at him with a 'well what?' look, then said, "Oh yeah. I love you too."

He kissed her. Her lips tingled. Her hands shook. Her legs weakened. She felt his love course through her body.

CHAPTER TWENTY-THREE

Skye called Gwen at eight thirty in the morning. "I'm sorry. I forgot to tell you that I'm meeting with a possible new supplier at nine fifteen, so I won't be in until at least ten, probably ten thirty."

"Why are you telling me? I'm off today."

"Are you serious? I can't believe I forgot. I'll call him and reschedule. I'm sorry if I woke you."

Gwen laughed. "I'm kidding. It's no problem. I got it covered."

"Remind me to tell you 'I hate you' when I see you later."

"You got it."

They hung up, and Skye headed out the door to her morning meeting at the diner. She preferred to meet potential business clients outside of the store. It forced the client to do their homework and couldn't just look around the store, acting prepared for the meeting.

Skye parked three stores away from Bric-A-Brac. She thought it was silly to park at the diner then drive four blocks to the shop. A man, with a few small boxes and papers spread on the table, sat near the back. She walked over and introduced herself. After she sat down, he gave his best sales pitch.

The sound of a fire truck passing stole her attention from the salesman. All she saw was the large red engine pass the plate glass window of the diner. Customers blocked her view to know if it was Engine 12 or not. She thought, "Be safe, JJ," just in case it was him.

Her meeting ended, and she paid for what she had ordered. The salesman insisted on paying, but Skye told him, "If I let you pay, I may feel guilty and purchase things I don't want or need. Right now, we're both still on equal ground."

The salesman complimented her on her business skills, "...especially for someone so young."

She left the diner and made the left to walk back to her store. She saw the fire engines three blocks away. Her walk quickened to almost a jog. When she got close enough, she saw the 12 on the front door of one of the engines across the street from her. She joined the handful of people who were standing in one of the lanes of traffic. The police had cordoned off both ends of the block.

Skye scanned the group of dirty yellow turn-out coats, he told her the name of the coat one evening, and black helmets for JJ. Her heart jumped when she spotted him. He was standing at an angle, speaking with another firefighter. She could only see a little of his face, but it still excited her.

Another firefighter walked in front of her. She bobbed her head left and right to see around him. He asked her, "Are you ignoring me?"

She looked up and saw JJ's eyes staring back at her. "Oh, it's you."

"Sorry to disappoint you. Were you looking for someone else?"

"Yes. I mean no."

JJ raised his eyebrows.

"I mean I thought he was you." She pointed across to the group.

He looked in the direction she indicated, but t couldn't tell which one she meant.

She stared at him. His helmet shielded his eyes, but not so much that she couldn't adore them. The chinstrap hung on both sides of his face; one end stopped just below his right ear, the other hung past his shoulder. The coat hung open, allowing everyone to see his chest in the dark blue shirt. *Oh my God, he's so sexy like this.*

"What's going on?"

"Gas leak."

"Is it going to blow-up?"

JJ laughed. "No. Someone left a valve open. We're airing it out now."

"Good."

"I have to get back. I saw you over here and wanted to say hello."

Skye moved to kiss him.

"I can't now. I owe you one."

She didn't like it but understood. Skye watched JJ walk across the street. The yellow coat hung low enough to cover the ass she loved to watch, and the pants were so bulky, she couldn't enjoy the view anyhow. He disappeared behind the fire engine.

Her cell phone vibrated; a text from JJ, "I love you." She looked for him but couldn't find him. She responded, "I love you, too!" She saw the time – ten forty. *Gwen is going to be upset.*

Before even checking for customers, Skye announced, "I am so sorry. I didn't intend to be this late."

"It's okay. I saw the fire trucks up the street. Is your honey there?"

Skye smiled. "Yes."

"Have you slept with him yet?"

Red coated Skye's face. "I can't answer that."

"Was he good?"

"Oh yes." Her smile broadened and face turned redder.

Gwen patted the stool next to where she was standing. "Sit down and tell me about it."

Skye sat down and proceeded to tell her about the date and spending the night at his place.

Gwen saw how much Skye smiled when she said his name. Like an older sister, Gwen touched her shoulder, "Is he *the* one?"

Without hesitation, Skye grinned and said, "Yeah, I think he is."

* * *

There was a smile plastered on Skye's face throughout the day. Gwen would catch her singing and join in, even if it wasn't what was being played on the radio.

Her happiness level dropped through the floor when Bart came in. His words the evening they met still stung. If people believed Rose was dead, then proving she was her, was going to be even harder. She knew it would hard enough to say, "Hi, I'm Rose." But saying, "Hi, I'm Rose and I'm not dead," was going to take a lot of proof.

Gwen reminded them both who the other was. Skye didn't need reminding, and Bart's words told her he remembered her, too.

"What are you doing here?" Gwen asked.

"My family is stupid."

"And you came here to share the news?"

"My mother got the bright idea of celebrating Rose's birthday."

Skye stopped filling-in an order form and stared at him.

"I could almost understand if it was her twentieth or twenty-fifth, but it would have been her twenty-third? It's like she's celebrating her kidnapping."

"You know your mom's heart is in the right place."

"Did I mention that it's a surprise party?"

"Are you expecting Rose to show up?"

"Yeah, I plan on her just bumping into her here in town, so I can get her there in time."

Gwen pointed at the door. "You'd better get out there then."

"I have to get her a present for her first. What do you get a dead twenty-three-year old?"

"A coffin?" Gwen laughed at her joke and Bart joined in.

They both looked at Skye who stared at them in disbelief.

Still laughing, Gwen asked, "What?"

"I just think that's a cruel thing to say."

"And why's that?" Bart asked.

"What if she's still alive and looking for you guys?"

Bart got serious. "You don't understand it. I've spent the last twenty years hearing about precious Rose from my aunt. My childhood was hell because my mother was afraid I'd be kidnapped. I'm over this whole thing, but my mother and Aunt Alice are keeping it alive. I think she's dead, just like the rest of my family. If she's still alive, she's doing a horrible job of finding us. It's not like Aunt Alice has made it difficult to find her. Her body needs to be found, so we can all go back to a normal life."

"It still sounds mean to me."

"Sorry Buttercup, but until you've lived it, you don't get a say."

You have no idea what I've lived.

"And just because you live in the house, doesn't mean you're entitled to an opinion."

Gwen chimed in. "Bart, you can stop now. She's a good kid with a good heart."

"I'm sorry. I didn't mean to upset you. I was saying…you know?"

"It's cool. I tend to overreact to this whole situation. I wish something would happen to put an end to it."

When I can find the proof, it will be over.

"What's the deal with the party? What kind of present do you need?"

"I need something that can be donated to the children's playroom at the hospital."

"Sounds like a stuffed animal to me. Over here." Gwen walked to the display, Bart followed, and Skye's gaze followed them, wishing she could find the proof she needed soon.

CHAPTER TWENTY-FOUR

Skye reread the four articles, hoping to find a clue she missed. Each one was the same, telling what Rose looked like, what her father looked like, and that her mother was distraught over her missing daughter. But she kept reading.

Alice Vandermeer met her estranged husband her freshman year at State College. They married two years later. She stopped reading and went back, *Alice Vandermeer met her estranged husband her freshman year of State College.*

"That's why I couldn't find him in the yearbooks here. He didn't grow up here." Skye walked to the refrigerator and got a soda. She continued talking to herself as she walked back to the table, "But how can I find out about him?" She set her drink on the table, flopped in the chair, then dropped her head into her hands. Tears of frustration ran down her arms. She looked up at the ceiling and cried, "Daddy why did you do this to me?"

An idea came to mind. She looked up the phone number of the college.

A lady's voice answered, "Hello, State College."

Skye replied, "Hi. I'm looking for some information about my father, but I'm not sure who I need to speak with."

"What type of information are you looking for?"

"Well, I'm not positive if he graduated or not and I'd like to know that."

"I'm not sure that information can be released. I'll transfer you to someone who might be able to help you."

Skye waited for the next person and went through the same conversation, who then transferred her call to someone else, and someone else, then another person. With the last person, Skye added, "My father died, so I can't get the information from him. I'm making a memory book and wanted the information for it."

"Oh, in that case, I can help you. I need your father's name and year of graduation."

Skye gave her the information and listened to the sound of her typing it into the computer.

"No, sorry. I don't see a William Maxwell and I checked the year before and after."

Afraid of giving herself away, but wanting the information, Skye asked, "Could you check for a guy my dad said was his best friend then?"

"Sure. What's his name?"

Skye took a deep breath. "Connor Vandermeer."

"Yes, he graduated with a bachelor's in graphic design."

Daddy was a graphic designer. "That's him. Thank you so much."

"You're welcome."

They hung up. Skye was shaking. Was this the clue she needed to connect her father to the kidnapping?

CHAPTER TWENTY-FIVE

Skye heard the familiar voice. "Sare?" She smiled as she heard the footsteps. She could tell where he was. "Sara?" JJ entered the kitchen. "Hey."

"Hi."

JJ looked around the kitchen. "Where's everybody?"

"Sara's upstairs. Abby made mud pies for dinner, so she's cleaning her up. Tyler's outside. I think he's lighting the grill."

"We're alone?" JJ walked toward Skye until she no longer had any personal space. Skye bit her lip, smiled, and nodded as JJ leaned in to kiss her. He didn't let go when he pulled back. "This is the official setting us up barbeque. It will be her and Tyler, you, me, and another couple. Then she'll suggest something that will make us team up."

"Doesn't she remember we met when you worked on my house?"

JJ kissed her. "She remembers. But she hasn't seen us go out, and we haven't said anything, so she's making sure we get to know each other better." JJ kissed her again.

"She's done this before?"

"I think she's set me up with every female in this town." He kissed her a third time.

A little voice interrupted them. "Unca JJ."

JJ dropped his arms, turned, and picked up Abby in one motion. "Hello, Princess."

Sara entered the kitchen. "Hey, when did you get here?"

"A few minutes ago," JJ replied.

Abby smiled. "Unca JJ kissed Miss Skye."

Sara moved her head backward. "What?"

"Skye had a hair in her eye she couldn't get. When Abby came in, she saw me blowing it out."

Skye nodded in agreement.

Disappointment overtook Sara's face. "Oh, okay." She redirected her gaze to the plate of sliced tomatoes. "That should be enough. Let's head outside." Sara grabbed the dish then turned to go outside. JJ, still holding Abby, followed a few steps before turning to let Skye walk ahead of him. She added some swing to her hips which made them both laugh.

When they got outside, JJ set Abby down. She held his hand and pulled him to the swings, so he could push her. Skye imagined him doing that for their daughter. "It's so cute how he is with Abby."

"Yeah, he spoils her. Whoever marries him is going to be a lucky woman."

Skye continued to watch them.

"My brother is a handsome guy, if I do say so myself."

"Tell me about your vacation. Did you have fun?"

"We always have a great time at the cabin. Even Abby relaxes some there. But enough about that, did I tell you JJ is a firefighter?"

"Yes, I joked about it with him the day he fell off the ladder."

Tyler laughed, "He fell off the ladder?"

"Quit it, Ty." Sara turned back to Skye, "Did you know he was Salutatorian for his class? He's really smart."

"I can't say that came up when he was painting my kitchen."

"You should spend some more time talking with him. I bet you two have a lot in common." She called to JJ, "Come here."

Skye admired the way JJ looked in the crimson polo shirt. She allowed her eyes to roam a little further south, too.

"What?"

"I was just telling Skye how I think you two would get along well. Why don't you take her over to the bench and chat while we wait for Chet and Lacy to get here?"

JJ rolled his eyes. "Skye would you like my sister to force you on me?"

"JJ!"

"I guess. I have nothing else to do before we eat."

Skye and JJ laughed when they heard Sara tell Tyler, "They have the same sense of humor. I think this time might work."

They sat down on a bench in Sara's garden. JJ told Skye to make sure she didn't look in their direction when they spoke because Sara was good at reading lips. He looked up and pointed to a cloud as he said, "I love you."

Skye looked to where he pointed. "I love you, too. How long are we going to hide this from your sister?"

"Does it make you uncomfortable?"

"At first, but now it's like a game."

JJ looked down and scratched his chin. "As long as you don't play games with me."

Skye looked at Abby. "The same goes for you."

"Sara hasn't taken her eyes off us." He waved to her. She turned her head as if she hadn't been watching them. They laughed.

Abby joined them on the bench. Sara called to her when she saw it, then told them the food was ready.

"I thought Chet and Lacy were joining us," JJ said.

Sara explained, "They called about ten minutes ago. They're having car trouble and don't know if they'll make it or not."

Sara arranged for JJ and Skye to sit next to each other at the picnic table. Abby climbed in between them.

Sara told her to move, but JJ stopped her. "If the Princess wants to sit next to me she can."

Sara agreed.

Dinner was enjoyable along with the conversation. Multiple times Sara referenced how nice it would be if Abby had a cousin or two. JJ reminded her, "By the time I have kids, Abby will be too old for them."

When it was time for Abby to go to bed, they moved inside. JJ read her a bedtime story. He rejoined the adults in the living room after he finished. Sara did her best to sing JJ's praises, who sidestepped the compliments.

JJ stood up. "Well, it's been fun, but I have to be getting home."

Sara tried to stop him to no avail.

"I was going to ask you to look at a leak I have," Skye added.

"Does it have to be tonight?"

"I have a date coming over tomorrow. It's an irritating noise."

Both Sara and JJ looked at Skye in disbelief.

"Yeah. Sure." He looked at his watch. "I've got fifteen minutes."

They said goodbye and walked toward Skye's house. When they were far enough that Sara couldn't hear him, JJ asked, "You have a date tomorrow?"

Skye giggled. "No, it was the only thing I could think of that made you have to come over now."

They were three steps into Skye's house before JJ grabbed her and kissed her. "I've been dying to do that all night."

"I've been wanting it, too."

JJ closed the door then led Skye into the kitchen, where he continued to kiss her. He pulled her close to him with one arm and held her head with the other. Skye's hands ran up and down his chest. She licked his top lip. His mouth moved to her neck. She opened her eyes, then closed them right away. He moved his hands down her back and grabbed her ass. She moaned.

"Can you stay tonight?"

"I can't. I work tomorrow."

Skye pushed her hands up his shirt. "Do you have time to go upstairs?"

"I don't. I have to go home."

Her hands moved from his chest to his crotch. "It's not unanimous that you leave."

"I know he wants to stay, but I got to go."

Skye frowned. "You sure?"

"If I stayed we wouldn't get to sleep until," he looked at his watch, "after one. Then I'd have to leave by six to get home and shower."

"You can shower here."

"My uniform's at home."

Dejected, she replied, "Oh."

JJ kissed Skye. "I'm sorry."

"It's okay." She took his hand and led him to the door. "Now get out before I change my mind and undress you right here."

He put his arms around her and dropped his head to hers. "You have no idea how tempting that is." His tongue darted out of his mouth, touched her lip, and returned to his. Then he gave her a goodbye kiss, a sweet, soft one. He whispered, "I gotta go."

"Bye."

Skye watched him walk out the door and down her walk. He looked back when he closed the gate. It was too dark to see his face, but her mind filled in the blank. She went to bed that night smiling, still feeling his kiss.

CHAPTER TWENTY-SIX

Skye looked at her clock – two twenty-seven a.m. Another sleepless night at the hands of her father's memory. Eyes opened or closed, she saw his face. She heard his voice, "I kidnapped you." She wasn't sure if her heartache would diminish. It was a constant stabbing in her chest. It felt so real, she panicked that she was dying. She refused to call for help. JJ was working, and she had never asked if her house was a part of his area. There was no way she could face him and explain what was happening to her. She decided if she lived until morning all would be okay. If she died, her problem would be over, and Bart would be right. Rose would be dead.

She tried to come up with ways to prove, or disprove, her father's words. She'd been to the library to look up articles. She didn't find her father in the high school yearbook. Skye verified that Connor Vandermeer graduated from State College, but without a picture of him, she wasn't sure it was him. The picture she had of Connor wasn't quality enough to tell if he was the man she called Daddy and drawing on it only destroyed it. If she could tell for sure without a screwed-up face.

Skye's memory drifted back to her twelfth birthday. The memory brought the sound back to her ears; the twisting metal, her father screaming, "No, no, no." But she could never remember her face hitting the dashboard. The pain she felt when she awoke the next day was never forgotten. Whenever the memory attacked her, the pain did, too.

Her father explained to her that she shouldn't panic when she saw herself. The bandages were because of her broken nose and right cheekbone. When they were removed, and the swelling had gone down, she spent countless days and nights crying that she no longer looked the same.

Her eyes opened as she sat straight up in bed. "My nose and cheekbone were broken. That's why I can't see any facial similarities." After she got used to the changes to her face, she never gave it a second thought. "That's why the age-progression pictures don't look like me."

Skye threw back her blankets and darted to the dining room. She pulled out the folder she was keeping all the information in. She flipped through the papers and pulled out the picture of Alice Vandermeer when she found it. "She has the prettiest eyes."

She was always told she had her father's eyes. "I guess they're right. I wish Daddy had gotten school pictures or took pictures of me when I was little, so I could compare my real face to these." Skye stared at her eyes reflecting. "Daddy always said he didn't buy them because they didn't show the real me, even before the accident. I wonder if that's what he meant." She bit her lip. It wasn't proof she could use for anyone else, but it made her believe her father was telling the truth.

The rest of the night was filled with sleeplessness. Skye laid on her back, then her side, she'd flip to the other side, then on her back. She even attempted sleeping on her stomach. Her hand fell asleep from in being under her. She didn't believe her alarm clock when it went off. "Ugh. Shut up." She slammed the snooze button three times.

When it went off again, she turned it off and grabbed her cell phone in the same motion. She called Gwen. Without a hello when she answered, Skye asked, "Hey, if I work for you on Saturday, would you consider working alone today?"

"Sure, girl. Not feeling well?"

"I couldn't sleep last night. I fell asleep about an hour ago. The alarm clock woke me."

"You get some sleep. And we'll talk about Saturday tomorrow."

Skye thanked her, hung up, and rolled over. She sighed. She wished her father was there to fix everything. She wished JJ was there to hold her. She wished there was someone she could confide in to get rid of the guilt and pain.

* * *

Four more hours of sleep didn't help much. But at least she could focus and didn't feel like she had been hit by a bus, how she had when she called Gwen. She considered calling her again to see if she wanted her to come in but decided against it. Five hours of work was too much to think about, let alone actually do it. She took a shower in the hopes of it waking her more.

She went over what had kept her up all night. Skye had avoided going to the police department to get the reports for fear of being recognized. However, her memory gave her reason to not be afraid. And if she were asked why she wanted the information, she'd just tell the truth, "I moved into the house where she lived, and I got curious."

She climbed out of the shower, dried her hair, did her make-up, got dressed and left her house headed to a place that held answers. But were they the ones for her questions?

The words she rehearsed on the drive to the police vanished with the question, "May I help you?" from an officer behind a chest-high desk.

Skye used her left hand to play with the fingers on her right hand. "I wanted to find out about looking at some old police reports?"

"How old?"

"Twenty years."

"That'll take some time. Fill this out." He handed her a piece of paper that looked like a job application. When she finished, she handed it to the officer. He looked it over. "You left the reason blank."

Her left hand was playing with the fingers on her right hand. "I bought the house where she used to live. I got interested in and wanted more information. Is that okay?"

"It's fine. Police reports are public record. We ask because of the stupid people who admit that they're going to do something illegal with the information."

She panicked. She didn't know if he was informing her or accusing, but her mind went straight to the accusation. "No, I'm just curious."

"Alright. We'll call you when we have it for you."

"Can I wait?"

"You can, but it will be about three days."

"Three days? Why?"

"The older reports are kept at a warehouse. The person who handles it goes twice a week. He went today, so he won't be going again for at least two days. And they're done in order. If he doesn't get to it, it will take longer."

"Okay. Thank you." Skye turned and walked away, chin in her chest. It was going to be a hard three days.

CHAPTER TWENTY-SEVEN

JJ's hands rested on Skye's shoulders. "Just put it in your mouth."

Skye looked up at him. "I don't know. I've never tried it before."

"Try it. I bet you'll like it. It won't kill you."

"You can't be sure of that."

"It's never killed anyone who's tried it on my watch."

Skye put the shell to her lips and released the substance it held into her mouth and let it run down her throat.

JJ moved to sit in the chair. "I told you, you'd like oysters."

Skye smiled. "You only got these because they're an aphrodisiac."

"I didn't think I needed one."

"You don't." Skye leaned in and kissed JJ.

JJ ate two oysters. "There's more if you want them." He pointed to the plate on the table.

"One more."

"I'm going to get dinner." JJ walked into the kitchen while Skye ate one more. He came back carrying two plates of Shrimp Alfredo.

"This looks good." She tasted it. Pointing to the food with her fork, and not even swallowing, she said, "This is so good. You made this?"

"Did I not mention I can cook?"

"This is amazing. You're a great cook,"

There was little talk while they ate, but the food didn't last long.

"You're a firefighter, handyman, and chef. What can't you do?" Skye asked.

"I can't bake. So, dessert is a chocolate torte I bought."

Skye snickered.

"What?"

"I expected you to say something manlier than torte."

JJ deepened his voice. "I got a multi-layer chocolate cake."

"Close, but something's still not right."

"I stole some sort of chocolate thing."

"There ya go!"

JJ stood and walked to the kitchen door. "So, would you like a piece of chocolate thing I stole?"

Skye nodded.

He disappeared into the kitchen, then returned with two tiny plates with a large slice of chocolate torte on each. "I stole the plates, too," he said as he set hers in front of her.

After dinner, they moved into the living room. JJ hit play on the CD player, then joined Skye on the couch. She cuddled under his shoulder and put her hand on his thigh. Her fingers made a squeezing motion, but all she was doing was feeling his muscular leg. They sat not saying a word, listening to the music.

Mid-song, Skye said, "Tell me about yourself."

"I already have."

In one motion, she sat up into a crossed-legged position, facing him. "I mean like your personal stuff."

"Like what?"

"What's your middle name?"

"Adam."

"And when's your birthday?"

"I was afraid you'd ask that."

"Why?"

"Because of when it is."

"When is it?"

JJ shook his head. "It's Thursday."

"Really?"

JJ's head moved up and down.

"I have to get you something. What would you like?"

"I'd like a box of nothing."

Skye leaned in. "Come on. What do you want?"

"I honestly don't want anything." He changed the topic. "What's your middle name?"

"Skye Lynne Maxwell." She smiled.

"And when's your birthday?"

Skye paused. "I don't know." *But I will when I see the police report.*

"You don't know your own birthday?"

"I thought you asked what I want for my birthday. It's April twenty-third." She lifted her hand to her mouth and bit a nail.

Skye thought about the police report; how it could answer so many questions. She knew it could hold the key to who she was. But she knew she needed more proof of who her father may have been.

* * *

Panic enveloped Skye when she saw the name on her phone, Centerville Police Department. Her first thought was that they knew who she was, and she should come to the station immediately. Her second thought was more realistic, that they have the police report waiting.

She answered. The officer on the other end told her the reports she ordered and were ready to be picked up.

"Reports? I only ordered one."

"Two reports were done for this case."

Skye thanked him and told him she'd be there later that day. She would be able to answer JJ's question from the night before honestly.

Even though she was going to pick up the reports, Skye still panicked that the officer would recognize her, different face or not, or that she would act suspicious and he'd figure out why she was there. She stared at the door, afraid of what was about to happen. Her fate, her life until this point lay on the other side. She took a deep breath before opening the door. The officer behind the desk welcomed her with a hello.

"I received a call saying the report I ordered was ready."

"Name? And I'll need to see an ID."

She gave her name. He opened a drawer while she searched her purse for her wallet. He pulled out a manila envelope, placed it on the desk, then compared the name on her ID with the one on the envelope. He asked her to sign a paper which already included the signatures of those who came before her.

This has got to hold the truth. Skye wanted to open it in there, but she knew the privacy of her living room would be the best. She drove home looking more at the envelope than the road ahead.

Skye got out and rushed into her house. She held the envelope to her chest as if she was hiding classified documents to take over the world. She flopped on the sofa and the envelope on the coffee table. She stared at it, shaking. *Please let there be information I can use in it.*

She ripped the envelope off the table and tore it open. She expected it to be one piece of paper, with just the information about Connor Vandermeer. It was much more.

CHAPTER TWENTY-EIGHT

Skye flipped through the pages. She read the first one. It gave Connor and Rose's information: He was twenty-six-years-old, five-foot-eleven inches, one hundred and sixty pounds, no facial hair and no glasses. She was three-years-old, thirty-seven inches tall, twenty-eight pounds, and no other identifying marks. And then the sentence that shocked her, "Minor has been missing less than twenty-four hours. Father probably got return date wrong. No further action needed."

The words stared at her. She reread the sentence. Then a third time. *If he had looked for me, I might not be in this position now.*

Skye went into the kitchen and got a glass of wine. She knew that was common back then, but it still upset her that she was ignored. "No further action needed? I needed help and he decided that my father just got the return date wrong? What did he think I was, a library book? Who does that? Why would anyone do that?"

Skye sipped her wine while she paced her kitchen, her breathing sounding like a dog's pant. Anger overflowed from her eyes. "Daddy and I could have been found and I wouldn't have to figure this out now." Her face dropped. "If we had been found, he would have gone to jail, and I probably wouldn't have known him." She sighed. "But I didn't know my mother because of him." She threw her glass into the sink, shards flew back at her. She turned and slid down the cabinets until she sat on the floor. "What did I do so horrible to be put in this position?" Tears fell into her lap as she held her forehead with arms braced on her knees. She knew once her father took her, there wasn't going to a happy ending for her.

It took a while for Skye to pull herself together. She stood up and turned to the sink. The remains of her wine glass sparkled as she washed her face. She didn't care enough to clean it up. Instead, she leaned, longing for her father's hug.

Skye turned and headed for the door. Grabbing her purse, she went to her car, hopped in and drove. She arrived at her destination. She put her car into park and stared, wondering if she had made a mistake, but she also knew that this was as close as she could come to her father's hug.

She got out of the car. Each step she took toward the house was filled with trepidation. She didn't know why she was scared, but she was aware of the frantic beating of her heart. She got to the door, turned to leave. *There is no reason to be afraid.* She turned back and knocked.

JJ opened the door, covered in dust. "Hey, what are you doing here?"

"I'm sorry. I'll go." Skye turned again.

He grabbed her arm. "You don't have to go. I just wasn't expecting to see you." He looked at her face. The red of her eyes told him she had been crying. "What's wrong? Come on in." He moved to let her pass.

She didn't move. "I can see you're working on something. I don't want to bother you." She hoped the tears she felt in her eyes didn't roll down her cheeks.

"Skye, get in here."

Her steps looked as though she was skirting landmines. She went to his sofa and sat down. JJ followed her.

"What's wrong?"

Skye looked at him. His eyes let her see his concern. "Please don't think I'm insane, but I need a hug."

JJ grabbed her and held her close. He kissed the top of her head. He smelled of sweat and cologne.

She tried to make herself believe she was smelling Old Spice, but the truth wouldn't let her lie pass.

"Do you want to tell me what's wrong?"

I was kidnapped by my father when I was a toddler. I'm Rose. Her tears made their way to his shirt. *I want to tell you. I need to tell you.* She sat up, looked JJ in the eye and said, "I was thinking about my Dad. I miss him so much. There's so much I want to tell him and things I want to ask him, but…"

JJ waited, but Skye didn't say anything else. She looked down. He lifted her face to his and kissed her. "Baby, I don't know what you're going through. Both of my parents are still alive, but I'm here for you." He gave a partial smile. "Do you want to tell me what you were thinking about? Is that what upset you? Or just in general?"

Skye shook her head and lied, "In general."

"Come here." JJ pulled her in closer. He held her until she broke away.

"Have you ever heard something about one of your parents and wondered if it was true?"

"Like what?"

"Something bad."

JJ snickered, "Like robbing a bank?"

Here's your chance. Tell him. Skye drew in a breath that more than filled her lungs. "Never mind."

JJ tilted his head to the side. "Did you hear something bad about your father?"

"No. I got something in my head because of something I read, and it was almost real. I just freaked myself out."

"Do you want some water? And I'm offering because I'm not sure what to say to that."

Skye shook her head.

"You hungry?"

"A little."

"I tell you what. I'll go take a quick shower, then we'll go grab something."

"I don't want to make you stop working."

"It's okay. I was going to stop soon to eat anyway." JJ stood up. "Give me fifteen minutes."

Skye curled her lips in. "Sure."

* * *

For the first time since meeting JJ, Skye was relieved when he didn't invite her to stay longer because of having to work the next day. She wanted to get home, to her own bed. But as she made her way upstairs, thoughts bombarded her already clouded head. *There's still the other police report.* She stopped midway up the steps and looked toward the living room. "I won't be able to sleep anyway." She went back downstairs.

The front page listed hers and her father's statistics, like the other one. *Nothing new there.* She continued reading, "Photos of both attached to last page." She turned to the back and saw the pictures she had seen a hundred times before.

Skye continued. She read about Connor Vandermeer's car, a blue Ford Probe. *Daddy liked those, but all of his cars were green.* She read about the business he owned, Vandermeer's Graphics. When she contacted the college, she found out about his degree, so this didn't surprise her. She learned that Connor had threatened multiple times to take Rose and never come back since the custody fight began. There was a notation that he had closed his business and personal bank accounts which meant he had over $100,000 in cash.

Then, Skye read the last line. Next to scars, tattoos, or other distinguishing marks, it said, "Large star shape under chin from being stabbed by a Phillips Head screwdriver. Skye knew that scar and knew it well.

"Daddy, what's this?" She pointed under her father's chin.

He laughed. "I was in shop class in high school. A friend of mine and I were sword fighting with screwdrivers. We had the really long ones." He held his hands twelve inches apart. "He jumped forward and swung his hand at me. I couldn't stop him, and he stabbed me with it."

"Does it hurt?" she asked as she touched it.

"Not anymore, but it did when it happened."

Skye thought hard. *He grew his beard not long after that.* However, whiskers wouldn't grow there, so she often played with it until she was too big to fit on his lap.

"Connor Vandermeer and Bill Maxwell were the same person." Tears flowed again. "I know that part is true. Now I have to find out if I'm Skye Maxwell or Rose Vandermeer."

Skye cried until she fell asleep on the sofa.

CHAPTER TWENTY-NINE

Skye's hair was not doing what she wanted it to do, so she gave up and put it in a ponytail. She stood in front of her door doing the last two loops before opening for it JJ. He stood laughing at her.

She opened the door. "You could have opened the door."

"You didn't say come in." JJ kissed her. "I enjoyed watching you. Where do you want to eat?"

"How about The Lake Front?"

"Sounds good. Ready?"

Skye turned and went into the living room.

"I guess that's a no." JJ followed her but was stopped when she came back out.

"I just had to get my purse."

They were walking to his car when Sara called to them.

"Ah shit." He turned to Skye, "At least she didn't catch us holding hands. What's up, Sare?"

"Where are you two going?"

"Skye wants new fixtures in her bathroom. We're going to the store, so she can pick out which one she wants."

"And you're going to help her? You're so sweet. Isn't he sweet, Skye, helping you like that?"

Skye nodded. She ran the palm of her hand over the top of her head. *Thank you, hair, for not cooperating or she'd know we were lying.*

"Yeah, I'm freaking amazing. Can we go now before the store closes?"

"You kids have fun."

"Shut up."

JJ walked to his side of the car, unlocked it, got in, then leaned and unlocked Skye's door. He watched her slide in. He looked and saw Sara still watching them. As he looked down to put the key in the ignition, he said, "Sorry I didn't open your door for you. She'll read less into it, if I looked rude." He put the car into drive, and drove off, waving to Sara as they passed her.

"I figured it was something like that."

JJ laughed and joked about what would happen if Sara found out they were dating as they drove to the restaurant. The joke that scared Skye was JJ saying how Sara would be at her house all the time, being nosy, trying to find out her secrets to make sure she was good enough for her brother. *I have to hide that folder when I get home.*

There wasn't a wait to be seated and ordered their drinks. Skye looked over her menu. JJ looked over Skye.

"What?"

"You look beautiful."

Skye rolled her eyes. "What are you getting?"

"Turned on."

She rolled her eyes again. "To eat?"

"The Shrimp Alfredo."

"I bet it's not as good as yours."

"Of course not. What are you getting?"

"The crab cakes."

JJ held Skye's hand while they waited for their dinner to arrive. "I love you."

She smiled. "I love you."

The dinner conversation surprised Skye.

"Did Sara or I tell you about the cabin we have in the mountains?"

"Sara told me she goes a few times during the year. But that's about it."

"It's beautiful. We call it a cabin because it's in the woods, but it's really a log house. There's a river near it, where we'd go swimming, when we were growing up. My dad and I go fishing there. And the view - fantastic."

"It sounds nice. I haven't been fishing in forever."

"Would you want to go with me for a few days next week?"

Skye smiled and nodded.

"Great. I'll put in to take off from work. You'll be okay with work?"

She shrugged. "Well, I own the place. I can always close it."

"How's Tuesday through Thursday?"

"Sounds great."

The waiter came by and asked if they wanted dessert. Skye ordered the key lime pie. JJ agreed and ordered the same thing.

Skye giggled while they waited.

"What's so funny?"

"Nothing."

JJ looked at her with a sideways glance.

He heard the wait staff singing their birthday song. "You didn't."

"Maybe."

Their waiter set a chocolate torte with a candle in front of JJ. He gave Skye a half smile and shook his head. When they finished, he shook his head again, then blew out the candle.

"Chocolate torte, huh?"

"You can have my pie, if you'd prefer it."

"No. When did you set this up?"

"I called this afternoon."

JJ shook his head again. "Thank you. And I'll eat the dessert you got for me."

Skye insisted on paying for dessert when the bill came, but JJ refused to let her see it. He held it in his lap until the waiter came by.

They took their time walking to the car. Their fingers were entangled. Every few steps, JJ would stop Skye to kiss her. She giggled before each one after the first one. And after each kiss, he thanked her for the birthday cake.

JJ unlocked and opened Skye's door. "Sara's not here, so I can do it this time." He kissed her again.

Skye grabbed him around his ribs and hugged him. "I love you."

"I love you, too."

They held hands on the drive back to Skye's house. "So, what if Sara is waiting for us?"

"I expect her to be waiting. I'll handle her questions. You just smile and look beautiful."

"How Neanderthal of you."

He glanced at her. "Can you name a faucet that you like?"

"No."

"I can. Shop talk will shut her up."

"Oh-kay."

When they pulled up to Skye's house, JJ said, "Since she's probably watching, I can't get your door for you."

Skye opened her door. "It's okay. I know how to work one." She looked around for Sara, then continued talking when he was a few feet away. "Tell me why you didn't kiss me on our first date."

JJ chuckled. "My mother told me to always open doors for a lady and never kiss her on a first date."

"That's a bit old-fashioned."

"Yeah, but I compensate by living the third date rule."

Skye unlocked her door then looked at him. "What's the third date rule?"

He moved his head backward. "You're joking, right?"

She walked into the house as she said, "No. What is it?"

"If you think the relationship is going someplace, you sleep with them."

She ran her finger the length of his torso. "I like that rule." She brought her arms up to around his neck and kissed him. "Go in the living room. I'll get us some wine."

"Going to get me drunk and take advantage of me?"

"You betcha!"

Skye got two wine glasses out of the cabinet. "Damn it. I forgot I'm out of wine." She went back to the living room. Her heart stopped when she saw JJ holding the folder with all of her information about her being Rose. "What are you doing with that?"

"It was on the sofa. I was moving it to the coffee table."

"How dare you go through my things."

"I wasn't going through it. I picked it up and the stuff inside started to slide out. I just tapped it to get the papers back in."

"Get out." Skye pointed to the door.

"What? Why?"

She hollered. "Get out of my house."

"Skye, I didn't look at it."

She screamed and pointed to the door, "Get out. Get out. Get out."

He walked to the door while asking, "Skye, what's going on?"

"How dare you go through my private things? Go away. I never want to see you again. I won't date someone I can't trust."

JJ held his hands up like he was being robbed. "I didn't go through it. I almost dropped it, is all."

Skye opened the door, "Get out and never come back."

JJ shook his head and walked out the door. He turned back, but Skye slammed the door before he could speak. She went back into the living room, so he couldn't see her through the window in the door.

Skye grabbed the folder and sat down in the chair. Setting it on her lap, she opened it. The papers weren't in a neat pile, how she kept them. She straightened them then closed it. She held it close to her chest, like a mother rocking her newborn, protecting it from the outside world.

CHAPTER THIRTY

A tap on the door interrupted Skye's dinner, not that she was really eating. Instead, she stabbed the food and moved it around the plate, while her thoughts were on JJ. She placed her fork on her plate. Her jaw moved twice as fast to finish the mouthful she was chewing. She stood up as she swallowed.

A young delivery man stood in front of her holding a large white envelope. "Skye Maxwell?"

"Yes."

He handed her the envelope. "Sign here, please." He handed her an electronic signature pad.

Skye glanced at the return address, one she didn't recognize, then placed the envelope under her arm. She did something that resembled her signature before handing the machine back to him. They both mumbled parting words as the delivery guy turned away and she closed the door.

Skye read the return address again, as she made her way into the living room, a lawyer's office in Santa Monica. Her mind went to the horrible things the letter inside could say. Panic traveled through her body. *If only I hadn't signed for it.* She flopped down on the couch. Both hands held the envelope as she read and reread the lawyer's name. Saying it out loud didn't change the situation. It only allowed Skye to hear the name outside of her head.

Common sense took over. She pulled the zip-strip to open the envelope. She found a letter and another envelope, which had a sticker with her name typed on it. Skye read the letter.

Dear Ms. Maxwell,

> *Enclosed, please find a letter, left in my care, by your father. He gave explicit directions to give this to you only after he has been departed for six months. Also, as per his instructions, the contents are unknown to me. This means I am unable to answer any questions you may have in regards to it.*

> *If there is anything else I can help with, do not hesitate to contact me.*

Sincerely,

Phillip Forte

Attorney at Law

Skye's body shook. She waited for the envelope to dissolve in her hands. When she was sure it was real, she opened it. Inside was a letter and a picture. She studied the faces which stared back at her. The image was Rose holding an Easter basket, her mother and father. She unfolded the letter.

> *My dearest Skye,*

> *Three days ago, I was told that I will not survive this cancer. The doctor isn't sure how long I have. He's guaranteeing six months, but could be as much as two years. When he first told me, my first thought was of you and how to tell you. I still haven't figured it out, so my Baby Girl, you are still clueless that I am dying.*

> *I have something I must confess to you because I can no longer carry the guilt. But I do not want you hating me in my remaining time. That would kill me faster. I may have broken down and told you, so the information I give*

you may not be a surprise. Or, I took my secret to my grave, and you are just now learning how horrible of a person I am.

"Oh, Daddy. You could never be horrible, and I could never hate you."

You have spent your entire life believing your mother died when you were born. But this is not true. I lied to you. I lied to everyone we've met since you were three-years-old. Three-years, four months, and twelve days to be exact.

Your mother and I were getting divorced. She threatened to never let me see you again when I refused to pay alimony. I could not fathom never seeing you again, when only seeing you on weekends was already killing me. When you visited me that weekend, I knew my only chance was to leave and take you with me. I could never tell you the truth. It would have been too much of a burden for you. My real name is Connor Vandermeer. You are Rose Vandermeer.

Skye read the next paragraph which stated her mother's name, the state, city, and address of her last know whereabouts – at least as far he knew. It was the house in which she sat. She read the last paragraph.

Skye, I hope one day you understand that what I did was because of a father's love for his daughter, not a way to hurt your mother. I also hope that when you understand, you can begin to forgive me for making you live your life without a mother.
I love you.
Daddy

Tears vacated her eyes like flames from a burning building and burned just as much. Her heart healed as it broke even more. She now knew that all of the information she had found was correct, and she knew who she really was. But the thought of her father thinking she could ever hate him ripped her heart out of her chest. She loved the man who was her daddy. And while she understood why he had done it, her chest still hurt from the pain of knowing he could have allowed her to know she was not motherless at some point in her childhood.

She went into the kitchen for a bottle of water. "I am Rose. I'm Rose. My name is Rose. I wish I could remember being her. I wish I knew what to do now that I have my proof."

CHAPTER THIRTY-ONE

Skye hit snooze on her phone again. She wasn't prepared to face another day. Another night of not being able to sleep made the idea of being pleasant to people unimaginable. When she did sleep, she dreamt about her father kidnapping her the way they're portrayed in movies – grabbing her off a swing while she screamed for her mother to help her. When she was awake, she replayed walking in and finding JJ holding the folder. There was no way to know what he had seen, and she wasn't going to ask him. She hoped to never see him again. She considered ending her friendship with Sara, but she knew she'd have to explain why.

At eight thirty, she sat up and called Gwen to tell her she'd probably be late. She looked around her bedroom, everything was the same, even though it was different. Life was pressing down on her. She thought she'd be happy when she found out the truth, but it made her feel worse. How could she tell her mother the truth? She had never given any thought to the fact that she would meet her mother before she had proof. *She knows how long I've been here. She'll think I'm lying or hate me for not telling her sooner.*

Skye willed herself to get out of bed and get dressed. JJ's face would pop into her head, and she'd shake it out. The few days it had been since she threw him out didn't stop the love. It just made her hurt more. It didn't matter where she was in the house, she pictured him smiling at her. She had to remind herself that smile held the teeth that bit her. *I wonder what he went through when he was working here, and I was at work.*

The drive to work tried to make her forget her life, but the stop sign she ran proved it wasn't doing its job. Luck was on her side, when she found a parking spot three stores from hers. Skye looked at her phone for the time, nine oh five. "Not too late."

Gwen and Quinn were holding each other, kissing, when Skye walked in. "Ick."

Gwen replied, "What?"

"Do you have to do that where people can see you?"

Gwen and Quinn's faces dropped.

"Not everyone wants to see that."

Skye walked straight to the office and sat in a chair in front of the desk. Gwen followed close behind.

"I quit."

Skye looked at her. "Why? What happened?"

"You're what happened."

Skye shook her head. "Me? What did I do?"

Gwen's voice mocked Skye's. "People don't want to see two women kissing."

"I didn't say that."

"The hell you didn't. I thought you were cool. I invited you into my home, but you're as close-minded as everyone else. It's only okay if you don't have to see it."

"I've seen you two kiss before."

"Then what made today different."

"JJ and I broke up."

Gwen sat down next to her. "I'm sorry. What did he do?"

"Why do you think he did something?"

"Because you said you two broke up, not he broke up with you. So, it must be his fault."

"I'm not ready to talk about it. Is that okay?"

"Of course, it is. And I'm here when you are."

"Go kiss Quinn and apologize to her for me for the misunderstanding."

* * *

Gwen did all she could during the work days to cheer up Skye, but the nights knocked her back down. Anything Skye did or thought reminded her of JJ or that she held the secret to Rose. *What if Daddy told Grammy and Poppy? They don't know I know, so they wouldn't tell me.* She dialed the phone.

"Hi, Grammy."

"Skye, Sweetie. How are you? It's been forever since you called."

"I know. I'm sorry. I've been busy."

"So, you found a job?"

Skye proceeded to tell them about buying the house and business. She avoided their questions about how much money she had left, by telling them about JJ.

"Is it serious?"

"We've talked about getting married and having kids, but that's it." She left out the part about them breaking up, so her grandparents thought she wasn't alone. "The reason I called is because I have a question. Did my dad ever say anything to you about doing something illegal?"

Skye could hear the shock in her grandmother's response. "Illegal? Oh no, your dad was a good man. Why would you ask such a question?"

Her response wasn't a lie. "I got a letter from a lawyer about Daddy." However, the rest of her answer was, "I think it's a scam to get some of his insurance money from me. I knew if anyone knew the truth, it would be you."

"I think the worst thing your father ever did was driving sixty miles an hour in a fifty-five zone."

After thanking them and a barrage of questions about her life and when she was coming home, Skye got them to hang up. She looked around the bedroom. *I really am alone. They love me, but I can never go back there.*

Skye got the folder with all the proof in it. She found the lawyer's name and phone number. Her hands shook as she dialed his number. It went to voice mail. "My name is Skye Maxwell, and I'd like to speak to Mr. Forte in reference to my father, William Maxwell. I'm interested in finding out if he has any more information for me." She hung up feeling even more alone.

* * *

Skye woke up, and for the first time since she started dating JJ, he was not her first thought of the day. She got through getting dressed, a toaster pastry, half a cup of coffee – the rest in her travel mug, and all the way to work without his memory playing games with her brain. When she remembered she had forgotten, *Damn statue of the firefighter holding the child,* she still declared it was going to be a good day because it was an hour and a half before she had her first thought of him.

Gwen called to her when she got there.

Skye replied then continued with the paperwork she had been putting off. She contemplated not ordering any more of the firefighter figurines but decided against it. She was strong enough to get through this part of her life and refused to let JJ win. She pulled her calculator out of her top drawer. Her left hand followed the list of numbers while her right hand input them into the calculator.

Gwen came into the office. "There's a guy here to see you."

"Salesman?"

"I doubt it. He doesn't have a briefcase."

Skye parted the blinds to see who it was. "Oh my God, no. Tell him I said to get out and never come back."

"Why?"

"Never mind, I'll tell him myself." Her legs threw the chair into the wall as she stood up. Before she was out of the office, she yelled, "Get out."

"Skye"

She walked up to him and pointed to the door, "Get out of here and never come back."

"If you'd just talk to me for a minute."

She walked, moving him toward the door. "No. I don't talk to people I can't trust."

JJ held his hands up, palms forward, in front of his chest. "I swear to you, I didn't do anything."

"You went through my private papers."

Gwen gasped at finding out what had happened to them.

He shook his head. "I swear I was just moving it from the sofa, so I could sit down. It slipped, but I didn't see anything."

Skye's faced narrowed. "You saw it, and now you're lying to my face about it."

JJ's voice softened, "Baby, I'm not lying. I don't know what's in the folder."

She opened the door. "Don't ever call me Baby again. Don't ever come back here. Don't ever come near me."

"What can I do to prove to you I'm telling the truth?"

"The only thing you can do is forget you ever met me. I'll be doing it when you're out of my sight." Skye pulled the door as if she was slamming it, but the double hinge prevented it. She stormed into her office. The bang of the door hitting the jamb satisfied her.

Gwen followed. "You okay?"

"Who does he think he is coming here? He never stepped foot in here when we were dating, but now he thinks it's okay? I swear, if you see him in here again, call the police. Have his ass arrested."

"You still love him, huh?"

"What? Hell no. Why would you even think that?"

"If you didn't love him, you wouldn't be this angry." Gwen crossed her arms.

"Yeah, well, maybe just a little. But I can't trust him. He went through my personal things."

"You can't love someone a little. Either you love them or you don't. And you are in love."

"That's beside the point." Skye flopped into her chair.

"Which is?"

"Never let him in here again." She stared at her feet then looked up and added, "Tell Claire I'm ready for her to find me my Mr. Right."

CHAPTER THIRTY-TWO

Looking at her face in the mirror, Skye wondered what she was doing going on a blind date so soon after breaking up with JJ. It had been almost three months. But to her heart, it was last week. When she broke up with her first boyfriend in high school, Grammy told her, "It takes just as long to fall out of love as it does to fall into it." *I still have another two months to go then.*

She got her phone out of her purse and called Claire. "I can't do this."

"Don't you back out now. You'll have a good time. I promise. Ted said Matt's a great guy."

"But JJ was a firefighter, too."

"You took one out for a test drive and liked it. Tonight, you'll see the one you're going to buy."

Skye laughed. "Okay, but you have to promise that if I'm not having a good time, you'll let me leave early."

"As long as you promise to stay all the way through dinner."

"Deal."

She hung up and said, "Hell, it's a free meal."

* * *

Skye arrived at the restaurant before Claire and her husband, Ted. The hostess offered her the option of waiting at the bar. "No, I'll just wait here." She pointed to a bench hidden in a cubby. Even if it was a Saturday that she would have stayed home and watched TV, she was reconsidering and wondering if she made the right decision to meet the guy Claire called her Mr. Right. She repeated, "It's a free meal."

They arrived a few minutes later. Ted checked the bar for his friend. "He's not here yet."

Claire asked, "Do you want to wait here or get a table?" It was directed at neither of them.

Ted replied, "Let's get a table. Matt just texted me. He's parked down the street and on his way."

The hostess sat them at a table near a window with a beautiful view of the wall for the arts and crafts store next door. For three seasons a year, there were plants and flowering trees to block the view. The winter offered six sticks pretending to be trees and a red-orange wall. They sat, Skye's back to the front of the restaurant. Matt would have the seat to her left.

"So, how's business?" Claire inquired.

"It's going well. We're in a lull now since it's right after Christmas, but I expected it."

"Here he is," Ted interjected.

Skye turned as Ted stood to shake hands with Matt. He introduced them as he released Matt's hand. "Matt, this is Skye. Skye this is Matt."

"Hello," Matt said.

"JJ? This isn't funny. I told you I didn't want to see you." She turned to Claire. "How could you do this to me? You knew I didn't want to see him again."

Claire's eyes widened as they filled with confusion. Ted looked at Matt, then back to Skye. He was as confused as his wife.

JJ attempted to explain. "No, it's not like that, Skye."

"I don't want to hear it." She ripped her coat off the back of her chair, grabbed her purse, and pushed past JJ. He followed her out the door.

JJ grasped her elbow. Skye shook off his hand before turning to him. "Don't touch me. Go away." Her voice elevated, "Leave me alone. Do you get it this time?"

"I didn't know it was going to be you. Ted said his wife wanted me to meet a friend. I was as shocked to see you as you were to see me."

"Right. If you didn't know it was me, why'd you use a fake name?"

"I didn't. Matt is my real name."

Skye rolled her eyes. "I wasn't born yesterday. Your sister called you JJ, not Matt."

"Matthew is my real name. JJ is my nickname."

"Oh sure. I can see how people got JJ from Matthew Waters."

"When I was little, I followed my dad everywhere. I wanted to be just like him. I would get on my bike and ride to the firehouse when he was working and hang out there. The firefighters started calling me John Junior because my dad's name is John. Then it was shortened to JJ. Anyone who's known me since I was little calls me JJ. The guys I work with know me as Matt. Because my sister introduced us, you were told JJ. No one lied to you or tried to trick you. It was just a mix up." His grey eyes connected with hers. She tried to look away, but they held her in place.

She wanted to still be angry. "Then why didn't you ever tell me?"

He shrugged. "It never came up."

"Bullshit." Skye turned away.

JJ moved in front of her, blocking her way. "When did you ever ask me my name?"

"I asked you your middle name."

"Yeah, you asked me, and I told you the truth, Adam."

Skye used her left hand to play with the fingers on her right hand. "When you asked me my middle name, I told you my full name."

JJ tilted his head to the right. "I didn't ask that. I already knew your first and last name. I only asked your middle name."

She looked him in the eye. Her mouth moved, but no words escaped. She knew he was right. She knew she didn't have a comeback. She knew she had to get away from him. Skye pushed past him.

JJ jogged past her to stop her again. "I never lied to you. You never asked me my full name, or my proper name. Hell, you didn't know what JJ stood for until I told you five minutes ago. You can't blame me for what you didn't do." He paused, staring into Skye's eyes. "So, tell me, Miss Skye Lynne Maxwell, if I cared enough to learn your proper name, why didn't you learn mine, when you said you loved me?"

Skye had no reply. He was right. His voice saying her name, "Skye Lynne Maxwell" bounced in her head. *My name isn't Skye. It's Rose.* She froze. She wanted to say, "You didn't lie about your name or who you are, but I've been lying to you all this time." Instead, she said, "Go to my house with me."

JJ's face tightened. "What? No. I'm done with this. You can go home by yourself. Wanting you to know the truth and wanting you are two different things. I'm going to have some dinner, get drunk, and forget I ever met you."

It was Skye's turn to stop JJ. "No, please. I want to show you something."

"Been there. Done that," he looked at her crotch, "And I don't have a need to go there again."

The pink of her cheeks deepened to a carmine. Her hands covered where his gaze met her body. "No, I don't mean that." Her eyes dropped. "Please go to my house with me." She used her left hand to play with the fingers on her right hand.

JJ released his frustration through his nose. "I don't know. I think I've had all the fun I can handle for one night."

Her fingertips touched his bicep. "Please."

He nodded. "But, I'm not kidding. If this is some ploy for make-up sex, I'm leaving."

"No, no. Really. There is nothing sexual about this."

JJ nodded again. "I'll meet you there in fifteen minutes."

Skye watched him turn and walk toward his car. Sweat escaped every pore in her body. She brought her hand to her mouth. "Why didn't I think before I spoke? What if he hates me more when he finds out the truth?" Her stomach churned. She was thankful she hadn't eaten anything yet, or it would be all over the pavement. Skye took two deep breaths through her nose. It was then she saw she had walked past her car. Her hand shook as she tried to open the car door. As she buckled her seatbelt, tears filled her eyes. She looked at herself in the rearview mirror. "This is it. The truth is revealed tonight. You will no longer be Skye. You will be Rose again."

* * *

JJ was waiting at Skye's house when she pulled up. She could see him in her rearview mirror when she backed up to park in front of him. Skye only used her mirrors, afraid of making eye contact with him. She couldn't tell if he'd been waiting long, but she could see he had time to undo his seatbelt and lean back in his seat before she arrived. His arms folded across his chest revealed more of the anger he still felt than the amount of time he'd been there.

When she got out of her car, she walked around the front of it. This way she didn't have to look at him. She wanted to look at him. Seeing him reminded her of how much she loved seeing his grey eyes stare back at her. Even when she heard his footsteps coming up behind her, she refused to turn around. Her heart jumped when he spoke.

His voice was toneless. "Okay, I'm here. What do you want me to see?"

She allowed herself to look at him. Thoughts flew through Skye's mind so fast she had to stop herself from trying to duck out of the way of the explosion of words - *Why did I tell him I'd show him? Now it will all be over. He is so handsome. Will he hate me now? I love his eyes.* She shook her head.

"You don't want me to see it now?" he asked as he shook his head.

"No. Why would you think that?"

"You shook your head when I asked what you want me to see."

"No, I was just...ah...I mean...I was getting a hair out of my face."

"Sure." His words said he believed her. His tone said he didn't.

Skye unlocked the door. Her heartbeat quickened. She was positive JJ could see her dress move with each beat. Her heart was hollering for her to turn back to him. Her head kept her walking upstairs to her bedroom to retrieve the file. "Go sit down. I'll be back in a moment."

When she looked into the drawer which contained the folder, she said, "It's time to do this. No matter what he says or does, it's time for the world to know who I am." She pulled it out and held her life story close to her chest. One deep breath and she took the first step toward her new life.

Skye came back into the living room. She sat next to JJ and handed him the file she had yelled at him about looking at three months prior. He reached for it and asked, "What's this?"

"Look at it."

When he saw what it was, he said, "You said you didn't want me looking at it."

She nodded. "I do now."

JJ sat back on the sofa, as he set the folder on his lap. The sound of his voice she knew so well returned when he asked, "You sure?"

Her head gestured it was okay.

Skye watched with terror and apprehension as JJ opened the folder. She used her left hand to play with the fingers on her right hand. He read the first newspaper article on top. When he finished reading it, he said, "I don't understand why you have me reading this. I know about it."

She pointed to the folder. "Keep reading. It'll make sense."

They sat on the sofa for almost an hour. Skye watched him read every word in her secret folder. Her stomach reacted whenever he looked at her while switching to the next paper. When he had two more documents to read, he confessed, "I'm sorry. I still don't see why you're having me read this. Everything in here is information that anyone who grew up here already knows."

Skye tapped the pile he hadn't read. "Keep reading."

"Okay." He picked up the next paper, read it, put it down, then picked up the last one. When he finished reading it. "I still don't get it."

She handed him an envelope. The only thing left untouched in the folder. "You didn't look at this."

JJ took it from her and read the contents, the words Skye's father had written. When he finished, he looked at her. Disbelief colored his face. "This is you? You're her? You're Rose?"

Hearing the words from someone else stole her ability to speak. Her eyes filled with the water she had held back for months. She moved her head up and down just once.

"I don't know how to handle this. Do you have any other proof? I mean, all you have is the articles and this letter. Have you done a DNA test or anything?"

Skye stood up and walked over to the fireplace without uttering a sound. She opened a box, then pulled something out. She watched the floor as she walked back to JJ then sat down again; her right leg bent under her, her knee inches from his. She took a deep breath. As she handed the picture to JJ, she said, "The lawyer, well, my dad sent this, too. He gave me this and I think it's my proof."

JJ looked at the picture. It was the original picture taken the same day as the one used in one of the follow-up articles; the entire town knew it. "This is you?"

Her eyes closed as she nodded.

JJ stared at it a moment longer. Then he put the picture on the coffee table. He moved his left arm to the back of the sofa. Skye focused her gaze on her knee that was on the sofa between them. "So, should I call you Rose now?"

Without looking up, she replied, "You're not angry with me?"

"Why would I be angry with you?"

"For not telling you sooner."

"You had to find out for yourself. I understand that."

Skye looked at JJ. "But I got mad at you for not telling me your name."

"That was a totally different thing. I've known who I am my entire life. You've just found out who you really are."

Her lips told her brain how much she wanted to feel his on them, but she resisted. "You're the first person I've told. Even my grandparents don't know."

"Real ones or the ones you told me about in California?"

"The ones in California. I don't know my real ones."

His arm moved from the sofa to her right shoulder. Skye looked at his hand. Its warmth spread through her body. "What's next?"

She looked him in the eye as she shrugged. "I'm not sure. I haven't thought that far ahead. I mean, I hadn't planned on telling you tonight."

The movement of his head acknowledging her comment was barely noticeable. "I think you'll have to tell someone soon. I'm not sure if I'm an accomplice now or not."

Skye laughed.

"I'm not joking. I may be considered an accomplice now that I know the truth."

Her gaze returned to her knee. "I hadn't thought about that. I'm sorry." She looked back at him. "I didn't mean to put you in this position."

JJ smiled. "I like this position." He kissed her.

As much as she wanted him to kiss her, she wanted to push him away, fearing this wasn't the right time. But his lips were soft and warm. They ignited her blood on fire. Her hands found their way to his chest. His hands found their way to her hair and waist. They made up for lost time, even though time stood still for the duration of their lips touching.

There was no rush. They kissed and kissed. Their hands moved but didn't explore. JJ removed his suit jacket when Skye moved to lie on the sofa, positioning herself under him. She unbuttoned his shirt and ran her hands over his chest. His hand found her thigh. It moved upward, raising the skirt in its way. JJ sat up to take off his shoes. Skye kicked off her heels at the same time. Both of his hands ran their way up her thighs when he laid down again. She poked him in the stomach with her thumbs, so he'd lift. He watched her hands as she unhooked his belt, unbuttoned his pants, and pulled down his zipper. They smiled at each other as their lips returned to touching. JJ removed his shirt, which brought Skye's hands back to his chest.

The front door echoed someone's knock. Skye's heart beat faster. She knew JJ couldn't have told anyone her secret, but her mind raced to that thought. She pushed on the chest she was just rubbing to be able to see out the window.

"It's Sara," she whispered.

JJ rolled his eyes. "She must have seen my car." Neither moved.

"We can't just ignore her."

JJ kissed Skye. "Why not?"

"Because she'll know why we're not answering."

Sara knocked again.

"I think she knows already."

Skye stood up, pushed her skirt down, then ran her fingers though her hair. "Do I look okay?"

"Beautiful."

She shook her head, both in response to his compliment and to get her hair to behave before walking to the door. JJ heard her open it. He grabbed his shirt off the floor.

"Hi," Skye said.

"Hey, I saw JJ's car out front and came over because I have a question for him."

He stood up and buttoned his pants and shirt. He pulled off his belt and slid it under the sofa.

Skye replied, louder than her normal voice. "Sure, he's in the living room."

Sara entered and walked into the living room. Her older brother stood before her, shirt untucked and no shoes. His usually perfect hair, mussed.

"What's up, Sare?"

"I was going to ask you a question, but I don't think I have to now."

JJ crossed his arms. "What's your question?"

Sara grinned. She rubbed her hands like a maniacal villain in a movie and stopping as though she was praying. "Are you two on a date?"

They knew how they looked. There was no use in lying. JJ smiled at Skye. "Yes, we are."

Sara didn't hide her happiness. "Is this your first date?"

"No, we've been on a few others."

"Are you two…like…a couple now?"

They looked at each other. They couldn't explain what had happened that evening. JJ replied, "If you don't leave, you could ruin that for me."

"Oh, oh, okay. I'm out of here." Sara hugged JJ before walking to the door, he and Skye followed her. She stopped and hugged Skye. "This is so great. I knew you two would hit it off."

JJ opened the door. "Yes, you did. Now go."

Sara beamed as she said goodbye and walked out the door. JJ closed it before she could turn and say anything else.

Neither moved. Skye wondered if Sara's interruption had put a stop to what was happening in the other room. She thought JJ had time to think about what she revealed. She stepped toward him. He put his arms around her as he kissed her.

"Do you want to continue this upstairs?" Skye asked JJ's eyes.

The right side of his mouth curled into a smile. "Yes."

Skye grabbed his hand and lead him to her bedroom. They continued the pace they had started in the living room into the early hours of the next day.

CHAPTER THIRTY-THREE

Morning light illuminated Skye's room. Her face and hand laid on JJ's bare chest. She lifted her head. He opened his eyes.

"I'm sorry. I didn't mean to wake you," Skye murmured.

JJ smiled. "You didn't. I was already awake. I was just lying here with my eyes closed."

"Good." Skye smiled as she kissed him then rolled out of bed.

"Hey, where ya goin?"

"I have to do something in the other room that I can't do in here." She exited the room.

He called after her, "But I won't be able to see your nakedness if you leave."

When she returned, JJ rolled out of bed.

"Where are you going?"

"It's my turn."

By the time JJ returned, Skye had put on a tee shirt and sweat pants and was almost finished pulling her hair into a pony tail, a hair tie between her teeth. JJ walked over and grabbed the other end of the hair tie between his teeth as he wrapped his arms around Skye. She giggled at his playfulness.

Without releasing the hair tie, JJ asked, "Why did you get dressed?"

Skye opened her mouth enough to release the hair tie. She hooked her finger through it as she replied, "It's nine thirty."

JJ still had his teeth clenched, refusing to let it go. "I didn't ask what time it is."

"I have stuff I have to do." She let go of the hair tie and retrieved another off her dresser.

He spit out the hair tie and put it with the others on her dresser. "I was thinking we could spend another hour or two in bed, then go get some lunch."

"I like the sound of that, but I can't. I have to run some errands since I'm off today."

"We can run the errands and then get some lunch."

"You don't have to."

"I know I don't have to. I want to. Now come back to bed." JJ led Skye across the room.

"I'm surprised Sara hasn't knocked on the door yet, asking why your car is still here."

He dropped her hand and shrugged. "What part of that sentence did you think would turn me on more; mentioning my sister or her coming here?"

"I'm sorry. I didn't…I mean…it popped into my head and out of my mouth."

"That ruined it." JJ put on his underwear. "I'll get dressed then we can run those errands."

"You really don't have to go with me."

JJ picked up his shirt off the floor. He pulled it on over his shoulders. "Unless you're trying to get rid of me, I want to go. I want to spend the day with you."

Skye slid her hands inside his shirt. "I've missed you too." She bit his lower lip.

"Ow."

"I'm sorry."

"Now you have to kiss it and make it better."

"You are like a child sometimes." She kissed his chin.

"Speaking of children," he grabbed her around the waist, "I want to have a family with you."

Skye said nothing. She cocked her head to the side.

"Hello?"

"Umm, I heard you." The air conditioner was still running. She could hear it, even over the confusion in her head. Yet sweat ran down her back. "What did you say?"

JJ smiled. "I said I want to have a family with you."

Skye remembered a scene from *Sense and Sensibility* when Elinor didn't understand that Edward was proposing to her. She didn't want to be Elinor. But JJ was only saying family. He didn't mention marriage. He didn't say move-in together. He said nothing but having a family with him. Her mind raced. The answer was there, but she didn't know what the question was. She looked into his eyes. Even when he blinked, her stare stayed true. His head moved, but their eyes remained locked. She knew she wanted to be married before having children. She considered herself old-fashioned that way. *How do I ask if he wants to marry me or just have kids?* Then she thought perhaps she was reading too much into it. Maybe he just meant in the future, not now.

"Are you in there?" JJ's words pulled her out of her thoughts.

"I'd like to have a family with you, too."

"Soon?"

"One day." She broke free of his hold and walked to her dresser. She moved the hair tie JJ had put there more onto the pile she had there.

He followed the five steps to the dresser. "Too fast? I thought after last night we were back to where we left off."

She didn't know how to ask him to clarify what he was saying. If he just wanted kids, she'd feel silly for asking about marriage. If he was saying he wanted to get married, she'd feel silly for not understanding and didn't want to make him feel stupid for not asking so she'd understand. But she could answer the question he posed. "No, not too fast. I was thinking the same thing."

JJ grabbed her left hand. "We left off talking about getting married and having kids one day. Are we back to there?"

Skye grinned and bobbed her head up and down. He got down on his knees. She cocked her head to the side. "What are you doing?"

"Skye Maxwell Rose Vandermeer," as though it was her full name, "when a man proposes he gets down on one knee, but I'm on both. Ever since the first time I saw you, when I came here about helping you fix up the place, I haven't been able to get you out of my head. When I fell off the ladder, I was watching you and not paying attention." Skye nodded. "When we broke up, I was lost without you. I'm on my knees because of you." Her smile faded. "I've been on my knees since we met. I would rather be on knees next to you, than standing next to anyone else. I want to marry you and stay on my knees for the rest of my life worshipping at the feet of the most beautiful, wonderful, bravest woman I could ever dream of meeting. Will you marry me?"

Tears rolled down Skye's cheeks. The words she wanted to hear JJ say were finally said. She felt her heart beat. She could hear her blood rush through her body. Her head bounced up and down. "Yes, JJ. Oh yes." She bent down and kissed him.

JJ stood up, still holding the kiss and drew Skye closer to him. He pulled back, but only far enough to look into her eye, noses almost touching. "I love you."

"I love you, too."

As if controlled by an outside force, they moved to the bed. Any clothes either of them had already put on found their way to the floor. They took their time, knowing they had a lifetime ahead of them.

CHAPTER THIRTY-FOUR

JJ took off work Monday to be with Skye when she made the phone call, to be her support system; something she hadn't had in a year.

Skye's hands shook as she dialed the number that was written on the paper. She set the phone on the table between them.

"I'm sorry I got you into this."

He rubbed her shoulder. "Don't apologize. I love you. I want to help you with this."

"I love you, too."

They looked at the phone when they heard someone pick up. "Law Offices. May I help you?"

Skye swallowed hard. JJ nodded 'go ahead'.

"Hello. May I speak with Mr. Forte, please?"

"May I ask who's calling?"

"Skye Maxwell."

"Will he know what this is in reference to?"

"I think so. It's about the letter my father sent me through him."

"One moment please." They heard a click then an instrumental version of a Beatle's tune.

"What if you're in trouble because I told you?"

"Then we'll ask him what I have to do to get out of trouble or I'll miss you while I'm in jail." He winked.

A male voice on the phone said her name. "This is Phillip Forte. How may I help you?"

"Do you remember who I am?"

"Yes, I do."

Skye squeezed JJ's hand. He squeezed back while he mouthed to her, "Go ahead."

"The reason I'm calling is, well, do you know anything about my situation. I know you said you don't know what was in the letter, but do you know anything?"

"Yes. Your father confessed everything to me years ago. He wanted someone to know the truth in case something ever happened to him. When he was diagnosed, he gave me the letter with the instructions of when to send it to you."

"Then it's true? I am Rose Vandermeer?" Tears filled her eyes.

JJ dropped to his knees next to her, holding her around the middle.

"To the best of my knowledge, yes you are."

"I have..." Her voiced cracked. "I have an important question to ask you then. I let my boyfriend, fiancé, see the letter and the picture you sent. Now we're afraid he's an accomplice. We don't want him to get into trouble."

"Don't worry. You're both fine. First, you told him, not your father. The victim of a crime can tell anyone who was responsible for the crime without said person becoming an accomplice. Your father would have had to tell him. And second, since your father is dead, anything he wrote accepting responsibility for the crime..."

Skye wished he'd stop referring to her father as a criminal, even though she knew he was one.

"...only means that the crime has been solved. So, you both are okay."

They sighed simultaneously before kissing. "Thank you, Mr. Forte."

"You're welcome. Is there anything I can help you with?"

"No, nothing else."

They said their goodbyes and hung up.

JJ was still on his knees next to Skye. Her arms wrapped around his head and laid hers on it. She whimpered. He held her. She looked at him, eyes red and cheeks wet from tears. "It's over. I know the truth. You know the truth. It's not a secret anymore."

"Skye, only you and I know. It's still a secret. There's one more person you have to tell."

"I can't do it. She won't believe me or will hate me for not telling her sooner."

"She's been waiting twenty years to see you again. She may not believe you at first, but you have proof. You can do a DNA test. But she won't hate you."

"You have to go with me when I tell her."

"Of course, I'll go with you."

Skye fell to the floor when she attempted to hug JJ. She held on to him as if he was the only thing on earth that could save her.

CHAPTER THIRTY-FIVE

Skye and JJ pulled up in front of Alice Vandermmer's house. JJ didn't have time to put the car into park before she said, "I can't do this. She's not going to believe me."

"You can do it. And I'll be there with you."

"I think I'm going to throw up."

"Just do it outside of my car, please."

"Thanks for the support."

"It's what I'm here for. Come on. The sooner you do this, the sooner it will be done."

JJ got out of the car, carrying the folder. Skye was out of the car before he got to her. She ran her hands down the thighs of her jeans. "Do I look okay?"

"You're look beautiful." He kissed her forehead. "You can do this." JJ took her hand and led her up the sidewalk.

Skye looked at the front door then JJ. "It's a surprisingly warm day. Do you think that's a good omen?"

"Knock."

"I don't see a car. She's probably at the restaurant."

"Knock."

Skye turned to JJ. "We should have called to make sure now was a good time."

JJ knocked.

"What'd you do that for?"

"Because you didn't."

The door opened, and Skye's stomach turned. She could feel her heart beat. Her vision blurred. She grabbed for JJ to keep from passing out.

"May I help you?"

This is where you speak. Say something. "Um." She glanced at JJ. He smiled and nodded. "Mrs. Vandermeer. I'm Skye Maxwell." She looked at JJ for emotional support. He squeezed her hand. "I own Bric-A-Brac and More."

Mrs. Vandermeer nodded. "I remember you."

Skye glanced at JJ again. "I was wondering if I could speak to you about something."

"I have to go the restaurant in fifteen minutes, but I have time until then." She came out onto the porch. "We can sit out here." They sat down. "Before you start, if this is in reference to the restaurant, I only talk business there."

JJ moved his chair right next to Skye's and put his arm around her.

"No, it's not about the restaurant."

"Okay then, what would like to speak to me about?"

Skye wondered if she should tell her or just hand her the folder. "Well, ah…" She got encouragement through JJ rubbing her shoulder. "…about Rose."

"What about her?"

Skye took a deep breath in and released it slower than normal. "I believe I know where she is."

"You and a hundred other people." She stood up. "Just call the police and they'll check your lead."

Skye jumped out of her seat. "No, please I have to speak to you about it. Please."

"What makes your information so special?"

She looked at JJ, who dipped his head. "I…Because…" She looked at him again.

"Go ahead, baby."

She used her left hand to play with the fingers on her right hand and took another deep breath. "I think I may be her."

Mrs. Vandermeer leaned closer. "Excuse me?"

"I believe I'm Rose."

Color drained from Mrs. Vandermeer's face. She pointed toward the street. Her volume raised with each sentence. "Get off my porch. How dare you? I don't have time for juvenile pranks."

Skye jumped up and down. "No, please. I have proof."

JJ moved to beside Skye. He held out the folder. "She has proof to back up why she thinks it."

She snatched the folder from JJ's hand. "If this some sort of joke, I swear I'm calling the police."

Like a lightning bolt, courage raged through Skye. "You can call if you want. If my proof is right, then they'll have to be notified." She offered her cell phone.

"You want me to call the police?"

Skye moved her head up and down.

Mrs. Vandermeer sat down. She opened the folder.

"Before you look at it, can I explain everything to you?"

"I guess."

"My father had cancer. One night he confessed to kidnapping me during a custody battle. They had given him strong pain killers, so I don't know if he was telling the truth or if it was the medicine. When he died, I came here to find out the truth."

"What was your father's name?"

"Bill Maxwell."

The color drained from her face Mrs. Vandermeer's face. She hopped up and headed to her door.

"No, wait. He said his real name was Connor Vandermeer."

Mrs. Vandermeer went into her house.

Tears filled Skye's eyes. "JJ?"

He shrugged, "I don't know."

Mrs. Vandermeer came back outside with a picture frame. "Is this your father?"

Skye studied the picture. Nothing about the man looked like her father. She judged his height by the women in the picture. This man wasn't tall enough to be her father. "No, it's not. Who is it?"

"It's my cousin, Bill Maxwell. He was on Connor's side during the divorce and custody battle. He left town a week or two before Connor took Rose. He had just turned eighteen. He kept in contact for about a year, but no one has heard from him since."

The mystery of the name had been solved.

"I've never seen him before."

Mrs. Vandermeer opened the folder. It held everything, Skye hadn't even removed the newspaper articles.

Skye used her left hand to play with the fingers on her right hand while she watched Mrs. Vandermeer leaf through it. After each page, she'd look at Skye.

JJ rubbed her back. She would look at him. Her face revealed how terrified she was. He mouthed, "It'll be okay."

When her phone rang inside the house, Mrs. Vandermeer waved it off. "The answering machine will get it."

Skye was shaking, and her nerves made it look like she nodded in agreement.

"I have seen all of this. None of it is proof."

Skye leaned toward her and flipped to the end, where the lawyer's and Bill's letters were. "Read these."

She read both letters. "Well then. It does seem like these letters are real, but you could have faked them."

Skye went through the proof she had, other than the letters. "Connor and my father were both Graphic Designers. My dad's favorite car was the Ford Probe. He told me he used to have one when I was a baby. And," she paused, "he had a star-shaped scar under his chin from a Phillips Head screwdriver."

Mrs. Vandermeer's eyes grew wide.

"And I have this picture the lawyer sent me." She turned to back of the folder.

"Oh my God! Where did you get this?" Mrs. Vandermeer picked up the picture of Rose holding an Easter basket, her mother, and father.

"The lawyer sent it to me when he sent me Daddy's letter."

She looked into Skye's eyes, "Rose?"

"I think so."

"I have to call the police."

"But I'm telling the truth."

"I know you believe you are. But it's been twenty years. As much as I want to hug and hold you, I have to know it's real."

"I understand."

Mrs. Vandermeer went into the house. Skye turned to JJ and sobbed on his shoulder.

"It's okay. It's almost all over."

* * *

Skye paced the small room in the hospital. After a barrage of questions from the police and having blood drawn, she was asked to stay. She wished JJ was there to get her through it, but the police were questioning him to find out his involvement. She flopped into a chair and held her head in her hands. An officer opened the door, startling her.

"What is JJ's real name?"

"Do you want to know what JJ stands for or his real name?"

"Tell me both."

"His real name is Matthew Adam Waters, but JJ stands for John Junior."

"Thanks." The officer closed the door. Her head dropped back into her hands.

She didn't even worry about looking up when the door opened again. She just waited for the next question.

"Are you okay?" JJ asked.

Skye looked up then jumped and hugged him. She sobbed on his shoulder. He held her, one hand between her shoulder blades, the other holding her head. He whispered, "It'll be alright. This will all be over as soon as the test results come back."

When she could speak, she looked at him. "But what if I'm not Rose."

He placed one hand on each side of her head and wiped away her tears with his thumbs. "Then we'll know you're Skye Maxwell."

"The police think you and I set this up to get money from Mrs. Vandermeer."

"I know. They mentioned it when they were questioning me."

She cried again. "I'm sorry I got you into this."

"Hey." JJ lifted her chin, so she'd look at him. "I'm here voluntarily. I've had multiple chances to walk away, but I promised to stay by your side. And I meant it."

Skye squeezed him.

They paced. They'd hug. One would pace while the other sat. They'd check the time on the clock on the wall.

"Why'd they take our phones?" Skye wondered.

"Probably to keep us from talking to each other when they separate us and forgot to give them back."

After more pacing and time dragging, the officer who had questioned them came into the room. "Ms. Maxwell, could you come with me?"

Skye swallowed hard. "Uh uh. Can JJ come with me?"

"Do you want him with you when you find out the results?"

"'Yes, yes, definitely." She reached for JJ's hand and pulled him to her.

They followed the officer down the hallway. He took them to a conference room. He opened the door. Six eyes were cast in their direction.

JJ whispered, "I feel like when I dream that I went to school naked, unprepared for a test."

Skye's eyes locked on Bart's. She nodded to let JJ know she heard him.

The officer told them to have a seat.

They hadn't had time to pull into the table before Bart pointed at Skye and said, "If this is some hoax you've put together from information you got from me, I guarantee I will make your life miserable."

An older woman slapped his arm. "Hush, Bart."

Mrs. Vandermeer said, "This is my sister, Catherine and apparently you've met my nephew Bart."

JJ stood and shook Catherine's hand. Bart shook his head no, refusing to shake hands. In a soft voice, Skye said, "Hi."

Both sides of the table spoke quietly to their selves. JJ held Skye's hand and brushed her hair out of her face. He pressed his cheek to Skye's. "I love you, no matter how this turns out."

She pulled back and looked him in his eyes. "I love you, too."

He hugged her.

An older doctor entered the room, along with a police sergeant and the officer who had been guarding them.

"I'm Dr. Chaffin." He sat at the end of the table. "I want to stress something before I reveal the results."

Bart chimed in, "It's like being on one of those mid-day talk shows."

Everyone looked at him with different stages of disdain.

Dr. Chaffin continued, "A DNA test cannot determine one hundred percent who a parent is."

Skye squeezed JJ's hand, afraid the answer was no.

"What it can do is disqualify someone as a parent or determine if the person is biologically related to the child."

Catherine interjected, "So if this test is positive, Skye is definitely a part of our family, but you can't tell us if she is Rose?"

"The higher the percentage, the more likely that the pair are mother and child." He looked around the room. "Any other questions?"

Some answered. Some shook their head. But all eyes were on Skye who used her left hand to play with the fingers on her right hand. JJ was still holding her right hand. He watched her hand instead of her face.

Dr. Chaffin looked at the paper again. "Skye Maxwell and Alice Vandermeer, are without a doubt biologically related." Everyone at the table looked to see how the other reacted. "You two are mother and daughter."

The only sound Skye heard was her heartbeat echoing in her ears. *I. am. Rose. I am Rose. I'm Rose.* She looked at JJ, "I'm Rose?"

He smiled and nodded. "Yes baby, you're Rose."

Still looking at him, she repeated, "I'm Rose."

When she looked away from JJ, Skye saw Mrs. Vandermeer weeping. She looked at Skye. Through her tears she said, "I've always known you were still alive."

Catherine was the first to hug her. "Welcome home, Rose. We've missed you."

Bart stared at her the same way he did at Gwen's the first night. Skye smiled at him and he smiled back.

Mrs. Vandermeer lifted herself from her chair and walked around the table. Skye stood. She wrapped her arms around her found daughter. They both held each other and wept.

* * *

News crews met the group as they exited the hospital. JJ held Skye's hand and she had her arm around her mother. The reporters bombarded them with questions. Bart spoke on their behalf. "My aunt Alice has been reunited with her daughter, Rose. Both will give statements after they spend some time together. For now, we're just thrilled to have Rose back home with us."

They thanked the reporters for being there, then headed back to Mrs. Vandermeer's house. The reporters followed them. They hurried into the house before they could hound them with more questions.

The five sat around the living room. Other family members arrived. All hugged Skye and asked the same question, "Do you remember me, I'm," then told her who they were. She had the same response, "I'm sorry. I don't remember anyone."

They all took turns asking questions about her life and her dad. "I'm sorry, but I don't want to discuss him right now. I want to get to know my family here." Then she'd ask a question to someone else.

"Mrs. Vandermeer, what would you like me to call you?"

She smiled. It was a gentle smile that reminded her of Grammy. "I'm hoping you will be able to call me Mom, but I understand if that's too strange for you now. Mrs. Vandermeer is too formal, though. Would you be comfortable calling me Alice for now?"

Once again that night, tears flowed down Skye's cheeks. "For my whole life I've wanted to be able to call someone Mom. It does feel strange, but I want to call you Mom, Mom."

"You probably haven't had time to give it any thought. Do you have a preference between Rose and Skye?"

"I'd like to use Rose, but it's too foreign for me. For now, I'd prefer Skye and see if we could move to Rose. Is that okay?"

She grabbed Skye's hand and squeezed it. "Of course, it is."

In the early hours of the morning, when exhaustion took over every emotion and feeling Skye had, she apologized and said she had to go home to get some sleep. Everyone in the room was yawning and understood. More hugs and tears followed as she and JJ left.

JJ called work to take the day off. As he drove Skye home, he told her, "I'm here as long as you need me."

She grabbed his hand. "I'm going to need you forever."

JJ brought her hand to his mouth and kissed it. "Have you decided which name you're going to use?"

Skye looked at JJ and replied, "What's in a name? Whichever name I choose, it would still sound as sweet."

THE END

Made in the USA
Columbia, SC
17 May 2019